Rth Rising

by
Donna Steele

Robert, could not have done this without you!! Thank you!! Donna Steele

All Rights Reserved

No part of this book may be reproduced or transmitted in any form or by any means, electronic or mechanical, including photocopying, recording, or by an information storage and retrieval system-except by a reviewer who may quote brief passages in a review to be printed in a magazine, newspaper, or on the Web without permission in writing from the publisher.

All characters in this book have no existence outside the imagination of the author and have no relation whatsoever to anyone bearing the same name or name. Names, characters, places, and incidents either are products of the author's imagination or are used fictitiously.

Originally published in 2012 by RIP but has been heavily revised.

Cover illustration copyright @ 2015
By Donna Steele
All rights reserved

ISBN-13: 978-1522786634
ISBN-10: 1522786635

Dedication

To Char – who dragged me along on this wild adventure and helped make it happen

And to Darwin – my best friend, lover and husband, who has put up with my mess all these years and made me believe I really was the strong women he saw, and that I could do it.

Rth Rising

Prologue

Glancing around to ensure he remained unobserved, Chi ducked into his office. He wasn't seen. No one hung around this late at night.

Usually being in the office soothed him. After all these years, the office reflected his personality—slightly messy, with lots of evidence of family. Holographic pictures of his beloved wife, Lil, his kids and his little granddaughter, Kat, adorned his large desk amidst the fragments of his programming. On the wall hung a photograph of his ancestral home from back on Rth. He'd never seen it. He'd never even seen Rth. He was one of the children born during the trip to New Home. But his parents remembered it, and their loving stories made it special to him.

Tonight, that didn't relax him.

His parents, part of the largest exo-planetary colonization undertaking planned in human history, ensured their progeny were well versed in what had happened back on Rth. No one who made the journey wanted humans to cause such an ecological disaster ever again. This group, at least, learned from past mistakes.

Chi Stans lived in the largest arcology on the planet; the first of the three to be completed. With the realization of its creators' dream, humanity could thrive in the perfect self-contained city and then venture into new areas of this world. Human life would thrive on the new planet.

At least they'd thought that was the plan.

No one should notice him back at his workstation, even though it was long after normal work hours. As head of the department, he often worked odd hours so he could spend time with his family. Lil's time, as a physician, was much harder to schedule. He took a seat at his access panel and logged in, pressing the gimp implanted in his wrist to the sensor so Puter would allow him access at his level. This work, definitely not authorized, caused him to be extraordinarily careful.

Unanticipated traps, their sole purpose to guard this one particular program, had greeted Chi from the beginning of this work. He moved at glacial speed to ensure the machine would pick up no alert. He'd left markers, things no one else would recognize, to ensure that nothing done thus far was spotted.

Or worse, undone.

When he began this hunt, almost on a whim, there had been no way he could have known he would find something of this magnitude, or hazard a guess at the time it would take to investigate it. He'd been on a personal, even selfish search, but vital in his opinion. Discovered by accident, this program and its implications eluded him at first. Even after he expanded his exploration, he'd not anticipated what it truly meant. The removal of this program, while essential, was proving to be harder than he could ever have imagined. Whoever installed this was good, possibly better than he was, but it must be removed. For the good of everyone, he needed to succeed.

Quickly he realized a major tangle loomed as his next obstacle, and began to carefully probe and test for a way to defuse it. After an hour, his eyes were grainy and he decided to call it a night. He didn't have the luxury of making a single mistake. He shook his head. Why did he have the feeling that time was running out? Puter wasn't some evil entity, only a machine.

Chi heaved himself up from the desk with a deep sigh. He would work on this again tomorrow, and every day thereafter until he completely removed all traces of the program.

At the door, he pressed his wrist to the pad to close down his access and secure the office. Instantly he felt warmth flooding up his arm. What was happening? The warmth grew to heat and his breath became labored. What—

He stumbled and fell against the wall.

As Chi slid down, unable to draw a breath, he realized his work had been discovered. Compromised.

Lil, he would never see her again. She didn't know his work. He'd never told her what he'd found. Would that keep his family safe? His little Kat, he'd been doing this for her, and for his daughter, Castra. What would happen now? Darkness took over his vision and the pain increased.

Lil...

Chapter One

Ducking behind the rubble from the construction accident, the young girl tried for invisibility. Her long dark blond hair escaped from the braid down her back and she knew her pants were ripped, but it didn't matter. Kat tried to assure herself she wasn't really doing anything wrong. Realistically, she knew she was supposed to be helping Mem with the housework. She hated doing the housework, and Gramma Lil was at an emergency, a *real* one. A worker had been injured badly enough to require Gramma Lil herself.

Other uninjured workers milled around, whispering about the legendary Dr. Stans and trying not to flinch. Kat could tell some of them wanted to help but didn't have the first clue what to do. A couple of them weren't even able to look at the injured man's leg because of all of the blood. Kat felt a measure of superiority. She'd seen Gramma Lil work lots of times and it didn't bother her at all.

"Kat, hand me the clotter." Gramma Lil's voice wasn't angry, only a little resigned.

Caught, Kat rose. No reason to make it worse by pretending otherwise. The others moved aside to let her through. She took the medium-sized blue jar of clotter from the special case her Gramma Lil carried and hurried over to the older woman.

Gramma Lil attached the numb cuff around the victim's leg. After it began to work, Kat knew she would irrigate the wound and disinfect it. The clotter would stop the blood flow and get some immediate antibiotics into his system. It looked like Gramma Lil would need to do something to close the wound as well. Once the numb cuff began working, the man relaxed, which brought his blood pressure down, and in turn caused the blood flow to slow even before the clotter could start to work. Gramma told her about that way back when Kat was just a kid.

"Okay, stay out of the way now, Kat." She watched as her grandmem turned back to the patient. After assuring herself the sides of the wound were together under the putty-like substance, Lil leaned back to work the kinks out of her spine and allowed the med techs to load him onto the transport.

Giving her patient a final check once he was settled, Gramma Lil sent them on to the hospital floor. Then she motioned for Kat to be quiet and follow her out of the area. The workers were already cleaning up the debris.

"Are you mad at me, Gramma?"

Gramma Lil shook her head. "No, I'm not mad but your Mem may be. She doesn't know where you are, right?" *No "maybe" about it*, Kat thought. Mem didn't understand she really needed to know about this stuff and wasn't afraid to go looking in order to accomplish it. Gramma Lil had made it clear that was their business. She understood how Kat really felt about lots of things.

Kat hung her head, guilty and repentant. Unfortunately, she and her Gramma Lil both knew she'd do the same thing again tomorrow if the occasion arose. Kat suddenly realized she was a mess and knew her mem would be appalled that she appeared out in public looking like this. Things like that mattered to Mem. Kat could feel her hair coming loose from her braid and her dirty shirt fell half out of the waistband of her ruined pants.

"I thought so. Kat, you can't keep on doing this."

"But I wanted to help you!"

Gramma Lil shook her head. "Kat, Puter will be deciding on your training area in just a few weeks. You can wait that long."

"Why can't I decide, like your parents did? I want to be a doctor, like you! I'd be a good one." Not quite a whine, but this was a conversation they'd had so many times before.

"This is not Rth, Kat," Gramma Lil said resignedly. "You know there are just a tiny number of people here compared to back there. We all have to do what's best for the colony. We've talked about this repeatedly. Puter is smarter than you, me or anyone. Your chromosome test will tell Puter what training to place you in, where you'd be best suited and the most help to the colony. You have to trust him. Besides, my parents didn't make their decisions when they were ten cycles old." She brushed back Kat's tangled blond hair, then held out her hand to her. "Come on; we have to let your mem know where you are."

They were both silent as they headed for the mover closest to Kat's apartment, anticipating the fight that would inevitably occur when they got there.

"Can I have one of your discs?" Kat tried to distract her.

"My medical discs? Why would you want one?"

"I want to learn it."

"Kat, I just told you—"

"I know, and if Puter says I can't be a doctor, I promise to forget everything. Please!"

Gramma Lil shook her head and squeezed her hand. "Come on. I'm sure you're already in enough trouble since you've been gone so long." They headed up with the others on the mover.

Kat looked down at her gimp to see how long she had been gone and winced. Yeah, Mem definitely would have noticed.

Once again, she wished her gimp could make time go slower. As far as she was concerned, it could do just about everything else. Gimp, really GMP, stood for Global Monitoring for Personnel; she'd always known that. She'd had hers since she was about ten minutes old. Everyone had one implanted in their wrist as soon as they were born. The children were taught all about them when they started lessons in the school. She didn't understand the global part but she knew Puter could monitor her and keep her safe through her gimp.

Weekly, she and her parents went to the station in their apartment and let Puter download their medical information and upload vitamins and stuff. When they ate at the hand food places, Da just pressed his wrist to the screen and the machine recorded the use of whatever they decided to eat.

Each morning as she entered the school floor, she pressed her wrist against the panel so Puter could record her presence and her health and all that kind of stuff. Even as a kid, she'd never worried about getting lost, because there were stations everywhere and she could just hold her wrist against any of them and read on the screen where she was in the arcology in relation to home. She'd wandered off a few times while exploring, much to her mem's dismay, but she always found her way home. The gimp made it easy. Getting lost was for babies, anyway.

The living areas were on the upper floors, ten and above. That's where she slept but not where she spent most of her time. She knew there were apartments for families of up to four, couples and singles interspersed on those floors for maximum efficiency. No space could be wasted; Puter was very clear on the subject.

The lowest floors held the manufacturing and recycling, with retail stores and food servers just above. Those lower floors were the most fun to explore because they were off-limits and she'd had to be sneaky about getting into them. Offices and work areas were below the apartments. That part was pretty dull but the hospital floor, the school and the nursery were on the top floors with the park on the roof. She spent most of her waking hours there.

As they approached her apartment, Kat's steps slowed and she looked up. "Gramma Lil, are you going to tell Mem I ran off again?"

"Do you think I'm going to have to?" Gramma Lil asked dryly as she pulled her pack closer. It was shift change and other commuters hurried past them to get to their own homes or appointments.

Kat's shoulders drooped and she heaved a put-upon sigh. "I just wanted to help you. When I heard there was an accident, I knew you'd be there. You're the best doctor there is and I wanted to watch you."

"I know you do, Kitten, but it's not a good idea. Besides, I don't want you to get your hopes up."

"But I'd be a *good* doctor, especially with you to teach me."

Gramma Lil only sighed.

Chapter Two

Davd Palfy wanted to pull the covers over his head and block out the sound but it never worked. Worried, he shoved his overlong hair out of his brown eyes. Mem was screaming and this time his da was yelling back just as loudly.

He'd learned a long time ago being out there in the middle of it did no good. He cringed involuntarily when he heard something hit the wall outside, then looked around to make sure no one had seen, even though he knew he was alone.

Nasty fights were common enough but this one seemed over the top. He was pretty sure Mem's consumption of the alco-drinks was basically at fault. Da got so angry when she lost control like that.

It became ominously quiet out in the main room. He lifted his head and wished he could see through the wall. What was going on? He jumped as the other bedroom door slammed.

Moving to his door, he opened it a crack. He could see no one out in the main room. Was Da gone? The other bedroom remained closed. Quietly he made his way to the main door and let himself out as silently as possible. He hesitated just outside but no movement came from the apartment. Now he needed to find Da. Where would he go?

Davd decided to check the garden first. They'd spent good times there and besides, he didn't have any other ideas. Relief flooded him when he spotted his da at the observation steps. Quietly he took his place beside him.

"Guess you heard all of that," Da said, not looking away from the horizon.

"Not the words. What's wrong?"

His da gave a bitter laugh. "The details don't matter, we just had another fight."

"I'm sorry—"

"Don't, Davd. None of this is your fault." He looked back out at the landscape. "It's not even your mem's, really. Maybe if we had more space…"

"Space? Do we need a bigger apartment?"

"No." The wave of his hand took in the forest in the distance. "Look out there, all of that land. That's where people should be living."

Davd blinked. "Outside?"

"Don't listen to me, Davd. I'm upset. Puter will decide when we move out." Davd looked up at him. He spoke the right words but they sounded funny somehow. Da's arm went around his shoulder and they stood silently looking out.

What had Da meant?

Chapter Three

Keira handed Lil a mug of hot toa. They both needed the caffeine. Keira took a seat at the table across from her.

The apartment, nearly identical to the one in which she and Chi had raised their children, was familiar. Their old place had been slightly larger; authorization to bear two children allowed them more space.

The furniture was no different than when Lil had set up housekeeping before Patik was born, black interlinking plastik. All furniture was mass-produced in the factories on the lower floors, but the colors of the cushions and decorations were left up to individual tastes. Everything served a multi-purpose, with the ability to fold into wall units for additional room when necessary. Space had been at a premium during the flight and they carried it over when the structure was converted into the arcology.

Lil looked around the great room, taking in the icy blue walls with pastel violet and white for the accents. The place felt cold to her.

The artwork didn't fit Lil's taste either. The colonists left Rth because of the damage pollution had done to the planet. The window inserts irritated and on some level offended her, showing pristine landscapes of the old world. If they hadn't destroyed Rth with their pollution and overpopulation, maybe some of that lovely landscape would still exist. To

Lil it was a travesty to display what had been so corrupted.

She displayed copies of some classic Rth art in her own apartment, though not landscapes, but she also enjoyed art created here on New Home. They would live out the rest of their lives on this planet, so in her opinion people should appreciate the culture they created here. Lil supposed Keira's decorations were calming on some level, and if she lived here, maybe she would need it.

Okay, that wasn't especially kind, but she had never been able to become friends with Keira. Maybe if she tried a little harder...

With an effort, Lil brought her attention back to the present. "I simply don't know what to do." Keira's frustration was plain in her voice and Lil knew she'd missed at least part of her diatribe. It wouldn't be hard to catch up. "Every time I turn my back she's gone. Should I follow her to the toilet? I can't even believe her when she says she's going there. She's too headstrong. I don't know how to handle her. This isn't what I— "

"It won't be long, Keira." Lil interrupted. She'd heard all of these complaints too many times. "The last DNA scans will happen this week." Lil carefully did not allow her impatience to show.

Keira nodded. "I noticed her friend Bree is in another growth spurt. Her whole class is growing so fast. I wish she'd act more like Bree, more proper, less reckless."

Lil nodded and decided to ignore the last comment. "Well, she should be in for the night. I'm going to get out of your way."

"You're welcome to eat with us." The invitation was tepid at best.

"Thanks," Lil shook her head. "I need to check on my patient, then I'm headed for bed."

"Lil," Keira stopped her mem-in-law before she got to the door. "Do you think there's a chance Puter will allow Kat to train as a doctor and make something of herself?"

"I don't try to guess what Puter will do. I'd like to think she'll have a child one day and follow in my footsteps, but I don't want to get my hopes up. Puter will check her DNA. We just have to trust it."

Keira sighed. "You're right. If you change your mind, stop back by and eat with us."

"Thanks," Lil managed to smile at her daughter-in-law. Keira rose from the table and put the cups in the recycler. She looked over at the door to Kat's room as Lil left the apartment.

"Make something of herself," Lil muttered once she was out of earshot. The woman was an idiot, despite her position in management in the retail section. To work off some of her tension, Lil went to the stairs instead of the mover. It was only a few flights.

The hospital, just below the school, took up three levels. The first level held labs and testing. This was where Kat and her classmates would come for their complete DNA testing before the final decision on their adult training. The second was used for minor illnesses, maternity and pediatrics, but Lil headed for the third level. Trauma and surgery were housed there, as well as more serious illnesses that needed quarantine facilities.

The rooms were a uniform soothing green, with calming art on one wall. Each room held four beds and full gimp stations were attached to every bed. With Puter to monitor everything, few personnel were necessary. An alert would be issued instantly if care were needed.

Lil's patient was resting with his leg elevated. The clotter had already been removed and the wound glued shut. He looked up and smiled when he saw her.

"You look like you're doing much better," she said, taking in his color and the fact there was no tightness around his eyes.

"I am, Dr. Stans. The name's Kyle and I'd like to thank you."

Lil took the outstretched hand he offered and shook it. "I'm Lil. Can you tell me what happened? I didn't take the time to investigate the scene, but I have to make a report."

He shook his head ruefully. "We weren't careful enough. We were moving panels to be stored below but we lost control of the mover. It hit one of the main walls and broke a couple of the panels. Some of the ends were sheared off and they went everywhere. One of them cut me as it went past. Let me tell you, I thought I was going to lose my leg for sure."

"It looked worse than it was."

"No, I believe you and that little girl saved me. Who is she? She sure was on the ball there. She handled things better than any of the adults."

Lil smiled at the compliment. "My granddaughter, Kat. I guess she was on top of the situation."

"You should be real proud of her. I bet she makes a great doctor someday. Puter could use more like her."

Chapter Four

Kat sat in her room, grounded and sullen. She would be allowed out only to go to school and back home. What she'd done wasn't so very bad, but Mem remained furious. Nevertheless, it had been worth it. Her shoulders relaxed a little and a smile formed on her face. She'd actually gotten to help Gramma Lil with a patient! Okay, only handing her the clotter wasn't that much help, but she'd known exactly what Gramma Lil was asking for and gotten it for her. And the blood hadn't bothered her at all. Puter must know her genes were perfect for becoming a doctor.

A quick glance ensured the door was closed tight. At least Mem never came in without knocking. Kat slid the disc she'd slipped out of Gramma Lil's pack from under her pillow. She needed to find a better hiding place, the *best* hiding place. Mem and Da sometimes went through her school bag and they would be angry if they knew she'd taken it. It was an older one; she purposely didn't take the newest one because it would be noticed too soon. She needed to study it now, so if Gramma Lil did notice, she could return it.

Kat looked around her room, trying to decide where would be the safest place to hide the disc. The room was identical in shape and size to her best friend Bree's, except for the decorations. Of course, her things were not kept as neat. Bree had helped her decorate her room with bright blue walls and colorful cushions, not at all like Bree's shades of pink

Where would Bree hide something so important? Her eye fell on the books printed out on real paper, gifts from Grandma Lil, *Grimm's Fairy Tales* and *Pride and Prejudice*. She didn't understand a lot in either book, but they were precious and just about the only things she made sure were kept in their proper place.

Yes, that would work.

Kat started to ping Bree and tell her about her adventure with Gramma Lil, but decided against it. Mem said grounded and Kat didn't want to make things worse. She set her wall screen for her math homework in case either of her parents came to the door, then slid the important disc into her reader.

"I won't do this every day," she assured herself. "I won't even carry it around with me. Mem never looks in my real books so it'll be safe there. I'm not really doing anything wrong. I just want to learn things. I can always slip it back in Gramma Lil's pack when she's visiting sometime. It's not like I'm going to hurt the disc." She nodded, reassured and settled back to study all of this exciting new information.

Chapter Five

Lil let herself into her apartment a floor below her son's home after checking on her patient. Kat truly did know how to help her when out on a call. The girl behaved as a real aide, not flinching at all from the open wound and knowing exactly what Lil asked for. The things she could teach the child.

No, she didn't teach. Puter continued to put her on the front lines. She was on the older side of the colonists now, but still sent on calls where field medicine might be necessary. Well, it did keep her skills sharp. She checked the gimp imbedded in her wrist for any updates on her patients.

Lil looked around the single apartment, small compared to the apartment her family inhabited for so many cycles. She'd moved here shortly after Chi died. Many things were packed away, even more given away or recycled. Family gatherings were held in Patik's apartment now, and that was fine with her. This compact apartment suited her. The colors, beige and green, were left over from the previous tenant. A bit drab, but she didn't spend enough time here for it to bother her. The only things that really mattered were the family photos rotating through her frames.

She was tired and that brought on loneliness. Lil dropped her pack on the table in the small eating area then headed for her bedroom. She stretched her neck and ran a hand through her hair, thick and dark blonde, like Kat's, but short enough to be out of her way as she worked. There were pale strands growing in it now, making it lighter, the color of white wine. At forty-seven she was a good-looking woman, tall and still trim. But oh she tired more easily these days.

She missed Chi. It didn't matter that he'd been gone for cycles. They had been meant to grow old together. He had been much too young to die. They'd known each other their whole lives. Fratz, but she waxed nostalgic when tired.

Puter put them together without even meaning to. Oh, no forced marriage, but they had known there was no one else for either of them.

Her daughter Castra tried, on occasion, to talk her into seeing other men. The very thought was repugnant to her. She and Chi had been more than contracted to one another; they were each other's best friend and confidante.

It had been a good life together, much too short, but good. A hundred cycles wouldn't have been long enough. Puter's decisions about both of them—sending her into medicine where she excelled in keeping the colonists healthy for decades now and Chi into programming where he could keep Puter healthy as well—had been stellar.

A husky boy, Chi grew into a bear of a man, large in both body and spirit, dwarfing her shorter, more delicate frame. His thick dark hair was wild, always looking as though he had just run his hands through it. His big laugh caused smiles and answering laughs from anyone who heard it. Memories of playing with Chi in the temporary village outside, before the arcology even became habitable, kept Lil company many nights.

He'd loved his children and Kat, putting their welfare and happiness ahead of his own needs at all times. In turn, everyone loved him as well. His death, so early, came as a blow to family and friends alike. Lil knew better than to blame herself, intellectually at least. She hadn't been there when he suffered his heart attack, but she would always blame herself for that lack of foresight. Chi exercised and took good care of himself. His genes were of the best, otherwise he would never have been on New Home in the first place, but she'd obviously missed something for such a tragedy to occur.

Patik took after his father. Castra looked more like her. But she had her father's sense of humor and enjoyment of the world around her. Castra's transfer to Thirdport had been hard. At least Patik, Keira and Kat were still close by.

Chi had been worried about something, under some sort of stress though he hadn't shared with her. She should have caught it. She should have urged him to confide in her. He'd returned to his office after dinner that evening to work on some nagging programming problem and never returned. Chi rarely discussed his work, putting it aside for family time. There was plenty to talk about without work. This problem bothered him enough to let it follow him home.

She pushed her memories of Chi aside.

Inevitably her thoughts returned to Kat. The girl was only a child and already showing such a talent for medicine. The only grandchild she and Chi would have, Kat was growing more than a little headstrong and today was just one example. She was adamant about following her own mind. Lil knew it was probably wrong to have told the child so many stories of Rth and her parents, but reminiscing with someone gave her so much pleasure.

Of the two children she and Chi had, only Patik was given authorization by Puter to reproduce, so Kat was the only one to carry on their family. Emotionless Puter made his decisions for the good of all, but it would be nice to have someone from her family continue here.

An MD and a geneticist, Lil's mother had inspired her own work. Her father, an engineer, was still spoken of with respect in some circles. Both of them were the best Rth had to offer in their fields and therefore recruitment for the colony became their reward. She shared those stories with Kat, maybe too often.

Everything had been shiny and new when she started school. The park on top of the arcology grew with her. The oldest trees the children now played under were her age. Kat always found that funny and begged for the story at every opportunity.

Why dwell on all of this? If a few minutes of working with Kat could cause such a mood, she needed to find a hobby. Briskly she pulled her pack toward her to see what needed to be refilled.

It took only a moment to spot it.

One of her discs was missing and she knew exactly where it was.

Chapter Six

Kat rang the buzzer to Bree's apartment and stuck her tongue out at the door's camera. Bree swung the door open and joined her in the corridor. "Come on! We're going to be late." Kat was already headed toward the mover.

"Since when are you so anxious to get to school?" Bree hurried to catch up.

"Don't tell anyone," Kat whispered conspiratorially.

"What?" Bree asked excitedly.

"I got one of Gramma Lil's discs and I've been studying it," Kat declared.

"You're not supposed to do that!" Bree whispered back frantically, looking around to ensure no one was listening.

"Then don't tell anyone." Bree wouldn't. They had known each other their whole lives and they lived just a couple of doors from each other. Each an only child, they were as close as sisters and spent most of their time together.

They reached the top floor and entered the school. It took up the entire top two floors and ranged in age from nursery to graduate school. Every class had room for at least twice the number of students.

Kat knew the sight of all the extra room gave Bree a lot of hope. Bree had confided in her long ago that she had no interest in whatever profession Puter chose for her. However, she desperately wanted to be allowed to reproduce, maybe even two children. Kat had never given that part of her life much thought. She knew Gramma Lil hoped for a great-grandchild since she embodied the last of her line, but it was too far in the future to think about.

Secretly, Kat thought Bree had a good chance. Not only did she love children, she was the prettiest girl in their cycle. Kat's hair was blonde, but Bree's natural curls glittered like sunshine. She looked after it better too, brushing it until it shone. Bright blue eyes, full lips and perfect white teeth highlighted her face. Surely Puter would want those genes to continue.

They took their seats in class and opened their small screens to math.

At lunchtime they headed for the roof, sitting in the shade of one of the trees closest to where the youngest children played. While they were eating, Bree looked around to make sure they couldn't be heard. "How did you get the disc?"

"Gramma Lil doesn't know. It's an older one, she doesn't need it."

"Neither do you. What if Puter finds out?" Bree whispered even though they were alone.

"How can he? Only you and I know. The stuff is so much more interesting than what we do in class. I promise I won't get behind, I'll only look at it after homework."

"No you won't," Bree said immediately. "You'll be looking at it every time you think about it, which will be all the time. You need to be careful."

"I will be."

"Why can't you wait? Puter will make the decision in just a couple of weeks."

"Like you're waiting? You've been volunteering in the nursery with all of your spare time," Kat retorted. "Besides, I want to already know stuff before I start the training. Then I'll be the best."

"You will be anyway."

Kat grinned. "Thanks. You'll be the best mother ever."

Bree looked down modestly, then grinned. "You're right. Puter has to know how good we are. He knows everything."

Kat nodded, very confident in both of their abilities.

After Bree left her to spend the rest of their lunch hour with the infants, Kat walked up to the observation level, the only place in the arcology you could see "outside." Kat rarely thought about the lack of windows in the apartments. Some people, like Gramma Lil, had famous works of art from Rth, others kept scenes of landscapes from Rth on their wall screens. If no preference was chosen, Puter displayed Rth scenery with New Home's current weather. Seeing outside for real felt good somehow and Kat took every opportunity.

Green flora stretched out as far as the eye could see. There were some open spaces in the distance, but vegetation of all shapes, colors and sizes predominated. Looking down on them from up here, not much ground could be seen because the growth was so dense. None of the trees looked to be even a third the height of the arcology, but she wasn't sure about that. There was nothing large enough to give much perspective.

Annoyed, she saw someone was already in her spot. She didn't recognize him. She knew all of the kids in her area by sight, but this boy was new to her. He looked to be about her age, with shaggy dark hair and disheveled clothes, as though he had slept in them. That gave her pause. No matter how angry Mem got at her, Kat always had clean clothes and plenty to eat.

He stared out at the trees and didn't notice her. Before she could decide whether or not to approach him, a large man hurried up. The man placed his hand on the boy's shoulder and he turned, then flung his arms around the man.

Kat moved closer, wanting to hear what they said.

"I'm sorry I wasn't at the shuttle when it arrived. I didn't get a call until—"

"At least she remembered to call you at all," the boy said, his voice flat. Kat revised her estimation. He seemed a little older than her after all. He wiped his nose and stood up straight. "I could've found you."

"I know. Tell me what happened."

"Da left. The contract wasn't quite up, but he broke it and left."

"I'm sorry."

"It's okay. I didn't want to leave her alone, but she put me on the shuttle. I wasn't sure she'd remember to call you. I need to get back."

"Give her a few days. This is a blow to her—"

"Why didn't she see it coming?" The boy's voice rose in anger now. "Why doesn't she stop drinking the alco-drinks? That's why he left."

Now Kat regretted moving in so close. She couldn't leave, not without being seen, and she didn't want that. This was private.

"You don't know why he left; neither of us do. If your da couldn't live with your mem, it's his decision. Did he ask you to go with him?"

The boy nodded. "How can I leave her alone? She needs someone to keep an eye on her."

The large man sighed. "It shouldn't be you." He reached for the boy.

"I'm never going to contract," the boy said fiercely.

"Don't say that. It's not the time to make such a decision. You know Puter has decided you're to have a son."

"No, I won't. Why should I, if I don't want to live with him or his mem?"

The large man seemed to deflate slightly. His arm went around the boy and turned him away from the trees to hold him tight for a moment.

From this angle, Kat could better see the boy's face. He had pretty eyes, with long eyelashes, almost as long as Bree's. He needed to gain some weight and clean up, but he was nice to look at. If he stayed here with the man, he'd be in her school.

He'd be above her, already in training since he knew he would have a son, but she'd still see him sometime. She knew without being told, that the information she'd overheard would have to be a secret, even from Bree. She wouldn't want to humiliate him. Knowing someone had heard this conversation would do just that.

"Where are your things?"

"I didn't bring anything. She didn't give me time to pack."

The large man muttered an oath, shaking his head. Finally they started moving away and she retreated around the tree to stay out of their sight. She hadn't caught a name, but it didn't matter. If he showed up at school, she'd recognize him. There was something about him that pulled at her, not pity, but...

Once they stepped on the mover leaving the garden area, Kat hurried to her spot and leaned over to look down at the wide swath of completely bare blackened ground around the base. Gramma Lil had told her nothing would ever grow there again. Some of the kids in her class said it also served as a barrier so nothing could sneak up on the arcology, but Kat dismissed that. Nothing out there could hurt the colony.

She wished there were nothing inside as well, as she remembered the boy's face.

Chapter Seven

The boy didn't appear again. Eventually Kat put him out of her mind. Hopefully he'd been able to return home and his mem was okay.

School was beginning to be boring. Like all the other students, she already knew that there were two other arcologies on the planet, identical except for size, one at each landing port. She'd never been to Secondport or Thirdport, but everyone learned all about them in school.

Designed with this plan in mind, the ships had been constructed in orbit around Rth because they were too big to lift off from the gravity. As soon as they landed here on M27-A, or New Home, a temporary village had been set up around the area that would house the spaceship-turned-arcology. She knew Gramma Lil and Grandda Chi actually lived in the village when they were little kids. Those stories were exciting, not at all the way Puter told it.

The blast of the landing itself had caused the landing site to be sterilized and hardened to support the weight of the structure. The huge construction equipment was offloaded and the ship itself leveled. The braking and landing of the craft had taken nearly as much fuel as the trip itself, since solar currents and gravities were used for most of the voyage. Kat didn't fully understand it the way her friend Mikeal did, but Puter said it was true, so she believed it.

The machinery and supplies they needed had been stored in the spaces below even the manufacturing area and that part of the arcology wasn't available to be explored. Kat knew firsthand, because she'd tried—more than once. She couldn't understand why everyone didn't try to sneak off and see the places that were off-limits. The colonists only converted some walls, hooked up the plumbing, installed the power source, and been in business. Of course months of hard work at each site was necessary, the building of the arcologies was part of their history lessons from the first day of school

Puter made it clear in every class that much of the work was completed back on Rth and those people should be given the credit. The planning of this colony had taken cycles and resources Kat couldn't imagine.

Just choosing this planet, M-27A, took all kinds of time and energy. Probes were sent out first to locate, then explore and catalog the planet.

The three moons that orbited the planet were a big part of the reason for coming here. They kept the atmosphere down, like the single moon of Rth. The smallest of the moons orbited several times a day and astrologers on Rth thought it would be gone before too many generations. The two larger ones were more stable and when they moved out of the arcologies to the seas on the planet, the tides would be like the ones they read about in Rth history.

Puter taught them no intelligent life or civilization was discovered on M-27A, but there were all kinds of wildlife. They consisted mostly of four-legged mammals that no longer came close to the arcologies. There were even pictures of some of them, taken before the colonists had moved back inside. The largest land animal the probes ever found were smaller than the extinct elefants of Rth. Some questioned the existence of an underwater civilization, but the probes had found no evidence.

The expectations of the dreamers on Rth were finally realized. M-27A truly was a stable, oxygen and nitrogen rich planet more than capable of sustaining a growing colony.

Nothing on this planet could harm them, and the harm done by humans on Rth was not being repeated here.

The problem was, she already knew all that stuff. She needed something new to challenge her. At least she had Gramma's disc, which she had memorized in no time.

Soon Puter would let her begin her training and she'd learn everything Gramma knew.

Chapter Eight

Wearing her very best dress, Kat waited impatiently for time to move faster. The dress wasn't comfortable, but this was an important occasion. She wanted to look nice; besides, Mem wanted her dressed up. She was going to graduate today and much more important, she would officially learn what her training would be. Her whole class had been escorted down to the first floor of the hospital area a few days ago for final testing. Their DNA was on file in Puter since birth, but a different in-depth test was performed this time with the sole purpose of finalizing where their true skills lay.

She pushed her hair back once more. It felt funny to have it down instead of in a braid. Blonde and thick, Mem said it was her best feature. Bree agreed and talked her into leaving it down for the ceremony. Bree knew more about those things than she did. She'd only balked at the idea of wearing a ribbon in it.

Da and Mem kept talking about how fast the time had gone, but she didn't feel that way at all. It had taken *forever* to get to this day. She knew her brain just couldn't hold one more math problem or history fact. She'd completely memorized the disc she had taken from Gramma Lil, but she still kept it hidden in her room. If she returned it, Gramma would know she'd taken it, right?

She was so nervous she couldn't hold a thought, except that today finally she'd know if she would be trained to be a doctor like Gramma Lil. Puter had to know how good she would be. After all those tests, he *had* to. And of course, Bree would know her profession too. Surely Puter would let her train for the nursery.

Gramma Lil was there, waiting to go to the ceremony with them. Her Aunt Castra wasn't able to attend in person. She had moved to Thirdport for the last cycles of her training, but she'd get the news through her gimp as soon as they did.

Mem checked her over one more time and smiled. "You look lovely."

Da nodded. "You certainly do. I can't believe you're already so grown up."

Kat's eyes shown, but she kept quiet. She didn't want to break her silent mantra. *A doctor, a doctor, please let me be a doctor.*

Da opened the door and they stepped out into the corridor where they met Bree's family. Her mem, Crystal, had Bree's hair. Today it was styled up in a fancy twist. Her da, Chark, was balding and grinning widely. Da and Chark shook hands.

The adults visited as they took the mover to the top floor. Kat and Bree were quiet; both too excited to have a conversation.

They stood in alphabetical order, smiling at their families seated in their old classroom seats. They would move to another part of the floor after this graduation for real training. It seemed to hit both girls simultaneously that they would be separated for large parts of the day now, and their hands clasped for an instant before taking their places in line.

As they moved up onto the small platform, Puter announced each student's future training. Kat wasn't paying full attention until Bree stepped up. She was too excited, but she snapped to attention when her best friend moved to the front of the line.

"43107BCK, Bree Kandal," the baritone voice of Puter said as Bree stepped up. "Archives."

Archives? They were sending her to work in the *library*? She could do that, but what a waste, was Kat's first thought.

"One child, male."

Bree finally seemed able to breathe again at those words. She could have a child, only one, but it was the most anyone had gotten so far. She couldn't really complain. She glanced over at Kat who nodded to her, then stepped down for the next student to take her place.

When it was Kat's turn, her stomach was churning. Gramma Lil was right; she *had* gotten her hopes up. When her turn came, it was all she could do to force herself to step forward. She took a deep breath and stepped up onto the platform.

"43035KPS, Kat Stans," Puter intoned. "Enforcer, no children."

Kat just stood there, shock overtaking her, unable to absorb the words. From what seemed like a long distance, Kat heard Bree gasp. Enforcer? She didn't know anything about the field. She'd never given it any thought at all. She managed to look up and meet Gramma Lil's eyes. They were full of tears and Da's arm went around her shoulders for support.

She stood there unable to remember how to walk. "Kat!" the boy following her whispered, bringing her back to herself. She managed to step off the platform and turned toward her seat. She saw the look of sympathy on Bree's face and looked away.

She didn't register anything until she saw Mikeal's shocked face as he stood on the dais. What had she missed? A wizard with numbers, Mikeal had been sure that Puter would put him in the engineering area. Kat looked over at Bree, who whispered, "agriculture," to her. Kat blinked. How could Puter choose that for Mikeal? It was even worse than enforcer.

It was wrong!

****

The luncheon planned as a celebration was much more subdued. Everyone gathered in Kat's apartment even though Bree's family tried to beg off. The food was already prepared. Kat and Bree sat silent, unable to eat. Kat could feel Bree watching her, but she couldn't speak.

Mem looked over at Kat as she laid the food out. "Kat, you're not a child. This is a good choice for you. It's a very prestigious position with a lot of room for growth."

Kat turned blazing eyes on her mem, but before she could speak, Da stepped in and pulled Mem into the kitchen.

After that, their parents and Gramma Lil left them alone. Gramma Lil was watching her, but she could only focus on the word "enforcer."

When she heard the communicator chime, she rallied for just an instant. Puter had made a mistake and was calling to explain, but it was her Aunt Castra calling from Thirdport, to congratulate the girls. It sounded to Kat like she was trying to sound upbeat for them. Kat knew through Gramma Lil that Aunt Castra had wanted children, too, but been denied, so maybe she understood, at least a little.

Kat shook her head when Da brought the communicator over to her. He didn't try to persuade her.

Gramma Lil took the call and spoke briefly with Castra then they ate a nearly silent luncheon. Bree and her family left shortly. Kat headed for her room. She heard Da start to follow her but Mem and Gramma Lil stopped him. She shut her door against the world.

****

Lil took the alco-drink Patik handed her and sank back into the chair. "She needs some time, Patik. This was a bigger blow than any of us realized. Let her be for a little while."

"She shouldn't have gotten her hopes up. She knew Puter would make the decision based on her DNA," Keira said, causing Lil to wince.

"She's only ten cycles old. I have to take the blame. This is my fault. I filled her head with tales of old Rth, of deciding for herself. I allowed her to accompany me on calls. At least I didn't send her away. She's good too, the best helper I ever worked with. She has a knack for it. I'm sorry, but it's true. I don't understand why Puter would make such a decision for the child." Lil seemed to huddle in on herself and shook her head.

"Don't you start questioning Puter too, Mem. He has no emotions. Everything is based on facts, logic."

Lil kept quiet. She'd heard those words so many times. It was said by rote now. Her son was right, but that didn't make her feel any better.

****

On the next school day, Bree waited in the hall for Kat to open her door. Kat hesitated for a moment when she saw her, but school wasn't a choice. She was ten now and training for her new career began today.

"Kat?"

"Let's go," she said dully and they headed for the mover.

"Did you hear about Mikeal?" Bree finally asked.

Kat shook her head.

"He was so upset, his da asked for a recheck from Puter."

Kat's head shot up. "Did it work?"

Bree shook her head. "He's going to be trained in agriculture but everyone feels like..."

"Like what?"

"Like you were both... robbed."

Chapter Nine

Mem and Da called her into the living room. More than a little confused, she stared at their serious faces. They waited until she was seated, then Da took her hand. "Kat, we need to talk to you."

"What about?" Kat looked over at Mem, but she wouldn't meet Kat's eyes.

"Well," her Da looked down, then back up at her. "Our contract is, it's time for renewal and we've decided—"

"You're splitting up?" Kat's voice was louder than she'd thought and she saw her mem wince. She jerked her hand from his grip. "Why?" She looked between them.

"You're not a child anymore, Kat. Your studies—" Mem started.

"Why?" she repeated.

"I've been offered a position in Secondport," Mem spoke up, finally looking at her. "It's a supervisory position, better than I would ever get here. Your da doesn't want to leave. You'll be in training for a few more cycles, but then you can decide if you want to stay here in Centerport or come live with me in Secondport."

"No, thank you," Kat said stiffly.

"We're trying to make this easy on you, honey. We don't want to disrupt your training. We thought—" Da reached for her hand again.

"You *thought*! Fine, go on thinking. You don't need me here to do that!" She stormed out, leaving Da reaching for her and Mem rising from the couch in a huff.

****

Lil let herself into her apartment, stopping short at the sight of Kat sprawled across her couch. "Kat? What's wrong?"

"Did you know?" Kat yelled at her.

"Apparently not. What are you talking about?" She laid her case on the table and hurried to Kat's side.

"Did you know about Mem moving to Secondport? That she and Da aren't going to renew their contract? Did you?"

Lil's shoulders slumped. "No. Kat, no, I didn't know."

"I thought... " Kat's anger seemed to evaporate, leaving only despair.

"I'm sorry, Kat." She started to say more, but instead just took her grandchild into her arms. Kat struggled for a moment, then gave in to the strength in Lil's arms and burst into tears.

When she finally got her composure, Lil handed her a tissue and brushed her hair back. "It's going to be okay."

"Yeah, sure. Mem's leaving, but Da'll still be here. That's what's important."

"Your mem loves you, Kat."

"Right, just like she loves Da."

"They've been together for a long time. They'll always be in each other's lives, because they have you."

"You and Granddad Chi stayed together."

"Things were different back then."

Kat started to speak and bit it back. "Maybe it'll be better. I can look after Da—"

"He's not your responsibility, Kat. He's a grown man. Let him be your da. You know I'll be here whenever you need me."

"Well I'm never going to contract. I can't have a child anyway, so there's no need. That way I won't get hurt."

"That's not the way to think about this, Kitten. They loved each other at one time, or they wouldn't have chosen each other to have you. And they have stayed together for cycles. They'll always have the best of their time together in you. Hold onto that."

Chapter Ten

Five cycles later

Despite the changes in their lives, which at times seemed overwhelming, Kat and Bree remained close. Nearly sisters, even though they no longer had classes together, they still lived across the corridor from one another.

Kat had grown tall and lean, her body muscular and firm. Bree wasn't as tall, more rounded, curvy. For a while, Kat had envied Bree her breasts. All the boys enjoyed looking at them and seem drawn to Bree, while Kat was treated as one of the boys, if they noticed her at all. Part of that came from her fitness training. She had to be able to press her weight in gym, run up and down two stories of the arcology without being winded. Having Bree's breasts would have been painful for that, she decided. Besides, the boys she knew weren't interesting and seemed to resent her brains.

Bree spent a lot more time at a desk, learning the systems for storage and retrieval of data. Whereas Kat envied Bree's figure and ease with boys, she found it funny that Bree envied her height and assured manner. Still, Kat knew they complimented each other. Bree always kept after Kat to accompany her to different functions and parties. The boys who constantly surrounded Bree didn't appear to mind, until they discovered Kat's training as enforcer. That seemed to intimidate most of them. Even when she did go along, the boys were always looking at Bree.

****

She'd avoided this for some time. Bree had regular appointments with the physicians in this section, but then Bree was to have a child when she contracted. It was a waste of time for Kat, but Puter had signaled a stern command, so here she was.

A nurse led her into a cubicle and instructed her to change into the paper dress. It wasn't cold, but she shivered anyway. She hadn't had sex yet, so that would have to be discussed. She didn't want to, it was fine for Bree and the other girls, but it didn't sound all that wonderful when the girls she knew talked about it. And they talked about it a lot. The boys in her training talked about it even more. She was already enforcer enough to know lies when she heard them, but there had to be some truth and she wasn't anxious to find out which was truth or not. Fratz.

She jumped when the door opened and berated herself for allowing her nerves to show. The doctor, a woman, only smiled. "This won't take long and you'll be back in class." She glanced down at her pad. "You've not come in before?"

"Uh, no need. I'm not going to reproduce."

"No, but your health is important. Are you sexually active?"

"No."

"Okay, we'll take care of that and add birth control to your gimp."

"Why? I mean, since I'm not going to reproduce, why don't you go ahead and sterilize me now?" It would make more sense. She wouldn't have to take the additional medicine.

"Oh, not at your age. Puter doesn't like to do that. If you were to reproduce, he might choose sterilization after the child was a cycle or so old, but it's better for you this way."

"Why?" It made no sense to waste the chemicals on her.

"If there were to be a catastrophe or a disease that attacked the population, we'd be able to rebuild. Puter has to think ahead and keep a contingency plan about everything."

She'd never thought about anything like that. Something could potentially wipe out the whole population? Probably everyone would be allowed to reproduce then, so she must be kept appropriately healthy as a backup. Talk about an ego boost.

The doctor regarded her curiously for a few seconds, then casually remarked, "You know, we could also do some enhancements if you like. I could increase your bust size and you'd only miss a day or two of school."

Mortified, Kat closed her eyes, but managed to shake her head. Why was everyone so interested in the size of her breasts or lack thereof?

She did not want to talk about this, ever. Not even to Bree.

The procedure that followed was mercifully swift and thankfully not too painful. Finally allowed to dress, Kat started to return to class but a disturbance caused her to look over at the far entrance. She spotted two enforcers half dragging a struggling boy. Was that Mikeal? What the fratz?

"Readjustment," an older enforcer said in a low tone to the attendant behind the desk. The younger enforcer looked over and spotted her trainee uniform. He nodded a quiet greeting. She returned it, then moved quickly toward the door. She hadn't given Mikeal any thought since that day. He'd been as upset as she'd been, maybe more. Now he looked feral. At least she'd been able to accept—

No, not accept, if she was honest but she'd been able to hide her feelings.

The look on Mikeal's face stayed with her for long time.

****

"Come on, Kat, it'll be fun."

"Fun? Sitting off to the side with a non-alco drink watching the boys try to get your attention?"

"It's not like that unless you make it that way. I know Asher is interested in you."

"Asher?" Kat rolled her eyes. "Yeah, I talked to him at the last party."

"Well?"

"He wanted to know everything I could tell him about you. He didn't specifically ask your measurements, but I'm sure he would have if I'd hung around any longer."

"Oh stop it. You're beautiful and smart and a lot of fun to be with."

"Give it a rest, Bree."

"Then come with me."

Kat sighed. "There's no reason to. You're going to make a contract, have a son. It's more important for you to get to know these guys, but I—"

"Stop it. There's no reason for you not to make a contract as well."

"Why would I do that?"

"Because you want to be with someone, make a life and a family even if you don't have children. Your Aunt Castra found a man she loves and she didn't have any children. She's very happy, you told me so yourself."

Kat sighed. Yes, she'd told her that and now wished she could take it back. Oh, it was true, Aunt Castra and Uncle Torr seemed very happy. But she didn't see it for herself, at least not with the boys she'd met thus far.

"So you're coming, right?"

"I'm not staying late. I have a presentation tomorrow."

"Fine. You'll have a good time, I promise."

****

I should have gotten that in writing, Kat thought as she stood watching the party from the sidelines once again. Maybe she should attend the parties the enforcer students held. She was always invited, but she didn't especially enjoy spending time after classes with most of them.

Maybe that was because it seemed most of those kids *wanted* to be enforcers, unlike her. They seemed to think it made them better or something, charged with upholding the law, forcing people to conform. On some level, it still rankled she'd been given no choice about this career by Puter. Forcing others to do what Puter decreed seemed hypocritical. Forcing? Had she said that aloud? She looked around quickly, but no one had noticed anything. She didn't talk about it anymore; it did no good, and only made her feel worse. She knew Gramma Lil was aware of it, probably Da, too, but there was no reason to belabor it.

That didn't mean it went away. She looked at the cases she studied with an eye toward injuries, infirmities, age, things Gramma Lil would watch for. No one knew she added in those factors when she was reviewing a case, but it sure seemed to make a difference, at least in her grade.

She watched one of the guys who had been hovering around Bree earlier. She thought he'd been introduced as Linc. Now he lurched into the wall a few feet away from her and careened into a table. Shaking her head, she rose and took the young man's arm. Way too many alco-drinks. As an enforcer-in-training, she should take him back to his apartment and make sure of his safety. His parents would be *so* proud, she thought sarcastically. Kat tried to catch Bree's eye, but she was too busy. Eventually she'd notice Kat's absence and probably be annoyed. Leading the unsteady boy out of the gathering room, she found a reader in the corridor and pressed his gimp to it to get the location of his apartment.

It wasn't that far away, so Kat turned him in the correct direction, grateful no one was around to witness this. When they arrived, the apartment was empty, so she pressed his gimp against the door and it opened.

She thought the walk sobered him a little; at least he was still on his feet. He turned toward her after they were inside and pulled her against him.

His hand roughly grabbed and kneaded her breast. She started to push him away, but stopped. Bree thought she needed to find someone, but Kat never bothered to look. She didn't really know anything about this and maybe now... besides, it was just sex. This idiot probably wouldn't even remember it. She certainly wasn't expecting someone to fall in love with her. She allowed his lips to cover hers in a slobbery kiss and tried not to flinch when he shoved his tongue into her mouth.

She allowed him to move her toward his bedroom with a fatalistic feeling, but it didn't matter anyway, right? Just get the experience behind her. He pawed her clothes from her body and pushed her down on his bed. Maybe he thought he was being romantic or seductive, but she felt like dough being readied to bake. She hadn't checked, maybe that was his training.

Kat nearly changed her mind when he tugged her pants down, but this was what Bree and the other girls talked about. There had to be something redeeming about the activity.

With no finesse, or foreplay, he shoved himself into her and she nearly cried out. Even with the medical removal of her hymen, it hurt a lot more than she'd imagined. She bit her lip while he used her as though she were a piston cylinder or something, slobbering on her breasts and murmuring words she didn't quite catch.

At least it didn't take long. He shuddered suddenly and collapsed on top of her. "Ah Bree, you're good. I thought your breasts were bigger." Then he was out.

Bree? He'd thought he was with Bree? Good Gault! With disgust, she disentangled herself from him and cleaned up, then quickly dressed and disappeared. She would never talk about this or do it again!

Even if he never remembered, no boy out there would ever be able to erase this from *her* memory.

Chapter Eleven

Davd held it together because there were too many people around. He was the man of the house, had been for a while now. When his da left the contract and moved to Secondport, Davd had wanted to go with him. He couldn't leave his mem alone though, so he'd stayed and tried to look after her.

He'd done the best he could, but it hadn't been enough. On those occasions when she passed out from the alco-drinks, he searched the apartment and emptied out all of the containers he found, those she tried to consume to the dregs as well as those she hadn't gotten around to.

It still hadn't been enough.

Puter gave her a new liver when she damaged the original one beyond repair. Strict warnings came from Puter that another slip would not be handled the same. For several months, she'd been strictly clean. Davd hadn't even realized it when she started drinking again. Subtle this time, she'd managed to maintain control for a while.

What would happen now? Davd looked up to see Ralt watching him. Thank Gault his uncle was here. Ralt was the one to bring the news, coming personally from Centerport so they wouldn't hear it from some stranger. Da was dead, killed in an industrial accident. Still crying, Mem was leaning on Ralt. Davd wasn't going to cry, not in public. These people were here to give them support. He could only hope it would help Mem.

He needed to get away for a little while. He looked over at Ralt. The older man nodded slightly. Permission? Whatever, he took it. Davd strode to the door, uncaring if anyone noticed.

Needing some fresh air, he headed for the roof garden. The small grove drew him as always. He took a seat leaning against one of the trees and let the tears come. He didn't know when it happened, but his arms were around the tree and he was sobbing into it. Da had been good to him, and stayed in touch, even after the transfer. Davd didn't really blame him for going. Mem was nearly impossible to be around when drinking. Now even that tenuous connection to sanity was gone. At least he had Ralt.

He fell asleep against the tree. That's where Ralt found him. The touch of a hand on his shoulder startled him awake. "You should come home, Davd."

Without speaking, Davd nodded and made it to his feet. "Is Mem okay?"

"She's asleep."

"Yeah, but is she..."

"I don't know."

"She always thought he'd come back. I think that's why she took the liver and tried to stay sober."

"Tried?" Ralt said quickly. He sounded shaken at the word.

"She's drinking a little bit. Not like she was before, but..." He looked up to see Ralt's eyes were closed. "I'm sorry."

Ralt's eyes flew open. "No, Davd, don't you ever apologize for your mem. She's made her choices. You've been the adult too early and too long. You should have called me."

Davd shrugged. "Most of the time it's okay. And right after the transplant, it was really pretty good. It just didn't last."

"She was never strong," Ralt mused. "When she met Sagan, she gave herself to him totally. He didn't want that much. I don't mean to speak badly of him, Davd, but he didn't love your mem the same. He wanted a short contract and a son, but not all the trappings of a full commitment. Your mem wanted someone to take care of her. That's not your responsibility. I want you to concentrate on your training. If it gets bad, let me know. You don't have to shoulder this alone."

"We'll be okay."

Ralt didn't correct him, just led him back to his apartment.

The arrangements made, Davd packed for himself and his mem. Ralt accompanied them to Secondport for the service. Da had never bothered with another contract. He could have no more children, so it wasn't really necessary. He was, however living with someone else, a woman named Mian.

His mem asserted her authority, as was her right being the mem of the only son, but did nothing to endear herself to the community in Secondport. Davd and Ralt kept quiet. It was Davd and his mem who scattered Da's ashes in the garden. Ralt stepped forward as though to help him support Mem's weight when she semi-collapsed afterward, but there was no need. Davd was nearly grown and he appreciated that Ralt didn't diminish him by forcing assistance.

Things spiraled down quickly from there. With Da gone, his mem gave up the pretense she wasn't drinking. Davd threw himself into his studies. Training as an enforcer, the career he had always dreamed of, he worked hard to be the top of his class. He tried to remain on the sports teams he loved, but more and more often, he was called to pick his mem up from some place or the other, forced to leave early. He knew the guys talked about it, probably sympathized or pitied him, but the topic became strictly off-limits.

Although Ralt called more often, Davd quit even trying to put Mem on the link. After a while, Ralt stopped asking for her, but the calls continued. He kept up with Davd's studies and life. Though it was never mentioned, both knew that eventually Ralt would be his family.

Davd began spending a lot more time at home. He could study there as well as anywhere, and it made it harder for Mem to slip out with him there. Two unexpected consequences were the result— she became craftier at hiding her stash, and women seemed to think him mysterious and therefore even more attractive than ever. Since approved by Puter to have a son, he'd never lacked for women in his life. He enjoyed sex and was good at it, if half of what the women told him held any validity. The problem was, they all seemed to be looking for just sex.

Of course, he'd seen what a contract could do to a "family," and he wanted no part of that. If he found a woman and wanted to be with her, then he would think about a child.

For now, well, sex drove away the thoughts of what awaited him at home.

Chapter Twelve

  After the fiasco with Linc, while not strictly avoiding Bree, Kat did spend less free time with her. It wasn't Bree's fault, she and she alone had made the decision to go with Linc, but the "you're good, Bree" was there in the back of her mind now and it was hard to completely forget it.

  Instead, she put in extra time getting some practical experience for her job. The training, in her opinion, left more than a few holes in her education. She began investigating areas of the structure she inhabited with a new eye. She often wondered and had on at least one occasion asked, why the training didn't include a visit to all areas of the arcology. The response—that it wasn't necessary if the job was done correctly—stung a little. Now her visits to non-public areas were done covertly, as they had been when she was just a child.

  Kat still didn't venture as far as she wanted, not allowing herself to be out of Puter's range for any length of time. Still, she felt she was a better enforcer for the extra knowledge, like carrying the emergency medical supplies.

  She realized Head was taking an active interest in her education and knew her by sight. If aware of her extracurricular excursions, nothing was said.

****

Cal brought Davd the news. Cal had graduated a couple of cycles earlier and was rising fast in the hierarchy of the enforcers. Always ambitious, Davd knew the man to be jealous of his luck with women as well as his grades and prowess in the games. With age his only obvious advantage, Cal used that on more than one occasion to lord it over some of his fellow enforcers. This time though, his expression was somber.

He walked into the classroom without a glance around. He just headed straight for the instructor. "Davd, get your things." The instructor said nothing more, but ice ran up Davd's spine. Cal still didn't look at him, but Davd knew.

He quickly rose, stuffed his reader into his pack, and moved to the front of the room. He followed Cal out into the corridor. "Mem?" he finally asked.

Cal nodded. "She's in the hospital. A friend found her..." He let his voice trail off. Davd headed for the mover, not sure his knees would hold out long enough to reach her, much less take the stairs. In the back of his mind the idle thought came, wondering if Cal volunteered for this assignment, then it was gone.

At least Cal didn't follow him all the way up here. The people at admittance recognized him and didn't try to slow him down. He received the room number and some privacy. Davd hesitated outside the door, then taking a deep breath, opened it and stepped inside.

His mem lay there, unconscious and hooked up to an IV and monitors. Almost immediately, a doctor arrived. "What happened?" Davd asked, his eyes never leaving his mem.

"Her new liver is shutting down. Davd, we warned her. Puter won't—"

"I know." This was what she really wanted. If she couldn't be with Da here, she'd leave. Fratz, she'd probably go hound him in some afterlife or something. Davd almost smiled at the thought.

"We can keep her comfortable, out of pain." Davd nodded. "We can also help her if you want to..."

Davd closed his eyes. "I need to call her brother. He's the only other family. I'm sure he can be here in a few hours."

"You don't need to make a decision today."

"May I stay here?"

"Of course. She'll probably wake up in an hour or so. We gave her something to relax her."

There was nothing to say to that. Davd took a seat beside the bed. He needed to call Ralt, but he wanted to talk to her first.

An hour later, she woke. Davd knew he shouldn't be surprised. Puter knew how to measure dosage.

"Mem? Can you hear me?"

"Davd, is that you? I'm sorry." She sounded groggy.

"Yes, it's me. Don't worry about anything now. How are you feeling?"

"Misty," she said with a faint smile. "I wish I could always feel like this."

Again no response was necessary. "I need to call Ralt."

"You shouldn't bother him, Davd. There's nothing he can do. Puter made clear what would happen if I didn't follow his instructions." She sighed. "I haven't been a very good mem."

Davd swallowed. Maybe she hadn't been what he would have chosen, but she was his, and his only parent now. Soon she would be gone as well. The doctors could make that happen in an hour or a day, or he could insist she stay around and suffer for maybe up to a week. He'd done his research. He knew what was coming.

"Ralt will want to see you, Mem. You don't want to deprive him of that."

She sighed and closed her eyes. "You're right, call him. He deserves a chance to say 'I told you so,' doesn't he?"

"That not what—"

"It's okay, Davd. He won't say it, not out loud. He needs to be here for you. Go ahead; I'm just going to rest my eyes now."

Davd waited until her eyes closed, then rose and made his way to the corridor with heavy feet. Pinging Ralt's private contact, he wasn't surprised when Ralt answered instantly. "Davd?"

"Mem's in the hospital."

"I'll be on the next shuttle." Davd could hear him barking for his admin to get him a seat to Thirdport immediately. "Are you okay?"

"Yeah. If you're too busy—"

"I'll be there as quickly as I can. I want to talk to the doctors with you." Davd couldn't reply and Ralt seemed to realize it. "Go home and change. You need to be comfortable."

"I don't want to leave—"

"She'll be looked after. It won't take you long."

Davd nodded wearily and after a moment, broke the connection. What else was there to say?

He did follow Ralt's suggestion and headed home. He peeled off his uniform and showered, then put on something more comfortable and headed back. He didn't bother to eat; the very thought turned his stomach.

Mem hadn't stirred while he was gone. The hospital personnel left him alone; aware that other family was expected. Davd looked up, surprised when Ralt entered the room. Surely he hadn't been sitting here long enough for a shuttle trip.

Ralt gave him a rough hug, then turned to look at her. "Has she been awake?"

"Not since I talked to you. No one's been in. I guess they're monitoring her out there. The doctor didn't ask directly but—"

"I know. We can talk about that in a little while." Ralt stepped closer to the bed. "Lia? Can you hear me?"

She stirred and after a moment opened her eyes. "Ralt? I'm sorry Davd disturbed you."

"He didn't. I wanted to come check on you."

Again that almost-smile touched her face. "Or to say goodbye?"

"Is that what you want, Lia?"

She looked away then. "Yes, it is. I'm only a burden to Davd and you. I was given another chance, I know and I messed it up too."

"You're not a—" Davd tried to interrupt.

She lifted her hand and put a finger to his lips. "You deserved a much better mem. Don't argue. We both know it. Ralt will be with you. He should have been the one to have children, not me. This will correct that."

"Lia—" Ralt started to protest, but her expression stopped him as well. He nodded. Puter had really made the decision for them in any case. No reason to belabor it.

The doctors were kind and did make her comfortable. Davd and Ralt were both with her at the end, and later, a private ceremony in the garden sealed that chapter of Davd's life.

His studies would become his top priority. His time with women was just that, time. No feeling accompanied the act. He'd gotten to the point where he didn't believe feeling even should be a part of the act. None of the women touched his emotions. Maybe that was the way Puter wanted it now. The population seemed to be decreasing, at least among the people he knew.

No one would miss it if one less boy joined the colony because of him.

****

Kat was surprised to find a personal invitation from Head to the enforcer graduation in her gimp. Of course, all students were always invited, but she had not attended last cycle. She would be graduating next cycle, so it made sense to go this time. She knew most of the graduates from Centerport and the celebratory party afterward would give her a chance to meet enforcers her own age from the other ports.

Head gave a short speech and distributed the small pin all enforcers wore. The uniform was what really identified an enforcer to the rest of the population, but the pin was always displayed on the lapel of the uniform jacket. She would be proud when Head pinned hers to that uniform, but would she ever not have a microsec of thought about what might have been?

The ceremony was short, then everyone moved to an even larger gathering room for refreshments and to congratulate the graduates. Kat took a cup of punch and hung around the edges. Head had asked her to be here, so she wanted to be sure to speak to him, but she never enjoyed this kind of thing.

She spotted Head across the room, and slowly began making her way through the crowd in his direction, stopping to speak to the graduates she knew. She had never realized all graduates came to Centerport for the actual ceremony. It made sense, who wouldn't want to receive their pin from Head? But it meant a lot more people than she'd expected. All of them seemed to want to speak to Head, which made for slow going.

Something caused her to look up and she spotted the man, officially her new supervisor. He was smiling, really smiling. That was certainly a different look on his usually stern face. He was speaking with a young man. The younger man wasn't one of the graduates. He was already wearing the uniform, but he couldn't be much older than her. Head laughed at something the younger man said and Kat took a closer look. She couldn't see his face well from this angle, but she could see the body. Nice, frakking nice in fact, with a tight butt and broad shoulders. He could be a poster boy for enforcers with that physique and easy manner. The conversation with Head didn't seem to intimidate him. His longer dark hair was barely regulation. She could almost hear Head now, demanding a haircut in the near future, and smiled.

Something about the easy grace of the younger man drew her, but after a moment, she shook it off. She wasn't interested, she reminded herself. Someone who looked like that would definitely be calling out Bree's name. She winced to herself at the thought. *Get the frack over it! It's over, it happened and nothing can change it. It needs to be in the past.* However, the thoughts of having to be introduced to him by Head caused her to pause. As though fate were on her side for a change, a number of people moved toward the two men, causing the line to grow. She used that to make her escape from the crowd.

****

Davd turned at the last minute and saw a slim young woman in a trainee uniform that clung to all the right places slipping out of the room. For just an instant, he felt the impulse to follow her. Where had *that* come from? He turned to ask if anyone knew her, but everyone was engaged in conversation.

He looked back and she was gone.

Chapter Thirteen

Da tried hard to make things more pleasant once Mem was gone. He'd asked for Kat's help with planning meals and they shared the little housekeeping necessary. He seemed constantly amazed at how fast Kat was maturing. He began asking more in-depth questions about her studies and fellow students. In fact, more conversation swirled around the dinner table than in cycles. Slowly Kat began to realize that the relationship between her parents wasn't what she, as a child, imagined it to be. They'd lived in a contract, whereas Gramma Lil and Grandda Chi loved each other.

They didn't discuss Mem, but they talked about everything else. To her astonishment, Kat learned that Da had wanted to be an electrician even less than she wanted to be an enforcer. A good electrician, programming had always been his dream vocation, to work with Puter like his father and sister. That had been an eye-opening conversation to be sure.

"Why didn't you ever tell me?" she stared at him in shock.

He shrugged. "I hoped you'd never have to know what it was like. When you had to live it too, I didn't see how it would help to know that I felt the same way."

"Does it still hurt?"

His smile seemed far away for a moment. "This is just between us, right?" Startled she nodded. "It would, but I, well I found a way around it."

"You did what?"

"I wanted to write programs and I do."

She sat silent for a moment. "You do?"

He nodded and smiled. "You remember Roge?"

"Yes, he lives a couple of floors up, doesn't he? He's the one with a different woman every..."

"Uh, yeah. Anyway, he doesn't like writing code nearly as much as I do, and after he's been with those different women, he's not always at the top of his game. We have an arrangement."

Kat sat with her mouth fallen open. "You're doing his work?"

"Yes," he said simply. "It's not exactly what Puter wanted, but the work's getting done and Roge and I both get what we want. Da taught me a lot, like Mem did with you. Of course Roge enters everything through his gimp, so..."

"So you're not interested in spending time with a lot of different..." Kat teased him.

Da laughed with her.

"Who knew my Da was such a rebel. I'm really impressed," she said, looking at him with new eyes.

"I'm not sure impressed is the right word besides, here I am confessing to an enforcer."

She laughed at that. "Don't worry. You're talking to a rebel enforcer, who equates medical information into her cases."

Chapter Fourteen

Kat would remember that night for the rest of her life. Only a few short weeks after that conversation, her world turned upside down once again. Da was gone, electrocuted in a freak accident that blacked-out a quarter of the arcology.

The door to the classroom opened and Head himself stepped inside. Her instructor came to attention immediately. "Sir, how may I help you?"

"I need to speak with," his eyes roamed the room and landed on her. Without another word, she rose from her seat. Obviously she was the person he had come to find. He nodded at her perception and held open the door for her.

"Is something wrong, sir?"

He hesitated, then nodded. "I have some bad news for you." He motioned to a bench in the corridor and with heavy steps, she allowed him to lead her there. He took a seat beside her, but didn't touch her.

"Da?" she asked and couldn't help the slight quiver to her voice.

He nodded. "There was an accident in the residential area. Puter discovered a problem, and your father drew the assignment. Nothing like this has occurred since the arcology has been inhabited. I will personally look into what happened. Your father was a good man. We knew each other slightly." Her head came up then. Da had never mentioned that. "And you're one of the best students to come through the program in cycles."

"Thank you," she said faintly, more out of habit than hearing his words.

He patted her shoulder somewhat awkwardly and seemed relieved when Lil came running up. Head rose and gave her his seat. "My deepest sympathies, ma'am."

She nodded, but her attention was on Kat. "Kitten, can you hear me?" She placed her hand on Kat's shoulder, bringing her back to them.

"Gramma?"

"Yes, I'm here."

"Uh, this is Head. He's in charge of the enforcers. He'll be my supervisor when I..." her voice ran out and Lil looked up at the large man hovering over them.

"Is there anything I can do?" he asked quietly.

"Thank you, but no. Is it all right if I take Kat..."

"Of course. Don't worry about classes the rest of the week. I know she'll have no trouble in that area. Please, be in touch if there is anything I can do."

Kat felt Gramma nod, but didn't speak.

After hesitating a moment, he nodded back to her and left them alone.

"Do you know what happened, Gramma?"

Lil shook her head. "I was on another call, so someone else... He's been taken to the hospital floor."

"I have to see him," Kat's voice grew stronger now.

"I know. Come with me."

Lil cut through the red tape of the hospital system to get them back to the morgue.

"Are you sure you want to do this, Kat?"

She nodded. Gramma Lil sighed and led her into the cold room. Da seemed to be resting on a table to the left. A white sheet covered him except for his face.

"He looks asleep."

Lil nodded. "Only his hand was burnt."

Kat stepped closer and touched his cheek. His face felt cold and he didn't, he couldn't, turn to look at her.

"Kat?"

"Did it hurt?"

"No, there wasn't time."

Kat swallowed and then it hit her, Da was Gramma Lil's son, not just her da. Gramma Lil was being strong for her. "Gramma, I'm sorry."

Gramma Lil looked up startled and tears formed in her eyes. Kat put her arm around her and they grieved together. Kat supported her from the room and accepted the condolences of her co-workers.

Then she led Gramma Lil back to the apartment she had lived in all of her life. Even as she entered it, she knew that too would end now. She couldn't stay here. She was slightly young to have an apartment of her own, but under the circumstances, she decided to apply. Maybe Head would be able to help her there.

She made Gramma Lil a cup of toa, then answered the door to Bree, Crystal and Chark. Crystal gave her a quick hug, then turned to Gramma. Bree held Kat, wanting to help, but finally admitting to her friend she didn't know what to do.

"You're doing it, Bree. Just be here."

Bree nodded and they watched as Chark answered the door for more people, friends who wanted to help them, be with them.

The next few days were a blur for Kat. Chark took over the arrangements. As a matter of course, the body was cremated. Kat and Gramma Lil, with Aunt Castra beside them, sprinkled his remains in the garden on the roof. Mem, Bree, Crystal and Chark accompanied them but stood back. Kat saw Bree crying but she stiffened her own spine, as she and Castra supported Gramma. She would not look at Mem, and her mem did not intrude.

After the memorial service, there was a small gathering in the apartment. Kat was mildly surprised to see Head there, but he had made himself available during the whole process. It felt good for him to take the time with his busy schedule.

Mem finally approached Kat. She could feel Bree move to stand close by for support and drew strength from that.

"Kat, I'm so sorry," Mem said quietly as she started to reach for her.

"Thank you," Kat responded, but took a step back, away from her hand.

"I—do you have any plans?" Mem floundered as though they were strangers, trying to make conversation.

"I'm getting a single apartment—"

"But you're not old enough. You haven't even graduated."

"Head took care of it for me. You don't need to worry."

"You *are* my daughter, Kat. I care about—"

"I know. I'm okay. You can go back home. Gramma Lil and I will look after each other."

Mem looked at her daughter and stepped back. "You can call me any time, if you need anything, Kat. I'll always be your mem."

Kat didn't bother to respond and Bree stepped up beside her. Kat turned away as she and Bree went to greet other guests. In just a few minutes, Kat watched from the corner of her eye as Mem let herself out of the apartment without another word.

Chapter Fifteen

Bree and Gramma Lil helped Kat move into the smaller single apartment that Head helped arrange. With his input, there had been no problem at all. Kat allowed Bree free rein in the decorations and managed not to cringe at the thought. She did know Kat's taste better than Kat herself at times. At least she knew better than to insist on pink as the predominant color.

The place felt right, snug even with all of the things she considered important arranged around her. The model of efficiency, this apartment definitely suited Kat. Bree had chosen a sage green for the walls and pictures by Monet to add the color. It did feel strange to be alone at night though. She and Da had fallen into a routine of having a quiet dinner or spending time together before bed, catching up with one another as they got used to being without Mem. She wasn't afraid, that wasn't the feeling. In any case she knew that Gramma and Bree were less than a ping away if she needed anything. It was just the disconnectedness of having no one to be with at the end of the day. She needed to accustom herself to it in any case. She never planned to make a contract, so this would be her life.

The oddest thing seemed to be leaving her apartment every morning and not have Bree across the hall. That took the most adjusting. With Da's death, all of the distance that had come between them vanished. Bree had never known the cause of it and now it was of no import.

A new wrinkle added itself to the mix with the incoming graduates from the different professions. A young man named Danl moved to Centerport upon graduation to work in the management section of facilities.

Apparently Danl took one look at Bree at a small gathering of the new archivists and never looked away. Kat hadn't been there to see it, but even though Bree seemed to be playing hard to get, it was obvious that the same thing had happened to her.

Now Kat was finally going to meet him. He'd been invited for a family dinner with Chark and Crystal. Pleased to be included, Kat said yes immediately. She looked forward to finally seeing this—in Kat's word —"paragon" up close and personal. The hard-to-get phase lasted such a short time, Kat wanted to laugh.

The pains taken over the meal and apartment amused Kat. Krystal's home always looked pristine, everything in its place, but tonight everything shone. Pillows were plumped to within an inch of their lives, even the chrome around the baseboards gleamed. Kat thought back to her own little apartment and vowed to try to at least try to get the scuffmarks off that area in her bedroom where she shoved on her boots in the morning.

The aromas coming from the kitchen were to die for as well. Known far and wide as an excellent cook, Krystal had outdone herself. Kat had eaten more than her share of meals here while growing up. Where Mem went the easy route, Krystal always experimented with spices and different ways to liven up the meals. No one ever thought of the recycled-ness behind the food when eating here. Kat always put that down to the fact that Bree's mem worked in the nutrition area, but tonight was way above even her standards.

Her internal laughter faded when she saw the man. He walked into the apartment and his eyes lit on Bree. The rest of the world disappeared for both of them. Obviously he was completely gone. Kat could feel it in the air when he looked at Bree, and Bree, beautiful as she had always been, positively blossomed under his gaze. Kat felt totally out of her depth.

Kat watched Krystal and Chark exchange knowing glances and felt even more left behind. Oh, she was happy for her friend but this was so much more than anything she had even imagined.

She returned to her apartment that night torn between panic and depression that she might never see Bree again. Her mind continued replaying the interaction between the two and she jumped when her gimp pinged.

"Kat, what did you think of him? I know we couldn't talk with Mem and Da there, but now that you've met him, I have to know what you think of him. Be totally honest, Kat. This is important." The words spilled out of Bree.

Kat blinked and found herself relaxing a little. "I think if he were any more in love with you, he'd implode."

Bree's laughter delighted her and Kat relaxed a little more. "Really? You're not just saying that?"

"Bree! You cannot tell me you don't see it. Frak, *feel* it. *I* was getting goose flesh across the table."

Again that delighted laugh, and Kat couldn't help joining in this time. "He adores you. I've never seen anything like it."

"He's so wonderful, Kat. I just can't believe how I feel when I'm with him."

"So what's the next step?" A long silence caused Kat's unease to reappear. "Bree?"

"He asked me to contract."

That knocked the breath out of her for an instant. "Already?" Kat counted back the weeks quickly.

"Yes."

"What did you say?"

"Yes," Bree's squeaked just a little.

"Gault! For fraking real?" Kat sat up straight now, everything else gone from her brain. Bree was going to be in a contract. They were still just kids, except of course, that they weren't. Bree had graduated; Kat would next week. She was already in her own apartment. But now she understood what Da meant about growing up so quickly.

"Is it too soon? Do you think I'm making a mistake?" Kat could hear the tendril of uncertainty in her friend's voice now.

"No, no, Bree it's not too soon. I should have had a vid on the two of you tonight so you could see how you are when you're together, how he acts when he looks at you. It seems right."

"Really?"

"Really. I can't believe we're already this age I guess, but we are. Bree, does he have permission to reproduce?"

"He does, a son, just like me."

Again Kat felt the wind knocked out of her. A child? Of course, since that had never been a possibility for her, she'd given it no thought. But Bree would finally be a mother, her ultimate dream. Well, it had been her ultimate dream before meeting Danl, now maybe they were neck in neck.

"Kat?"

"I'm here, just trying to absorb in all."

"I wish you could do this with me," her voice sounded slightly wistful at those words.

"Me? A mother? Yeah, right. No, you do that and I'll be the loving aunt who doesn't have the responsibility and can spoil him all I want to."

"You will too, won't you? Oh Kat, I can't believe it."

"*You* can't believe it. I just met Danl. Of course, he is all I've heard about for the past few weeks."

"I haven't talked about him that much!" Bree protested.

"No, you stopped for breath a time or two," Kat teased and Bree laughed again.

"Tonight he met the parents; now he and I want to have dinner with just you this week. Sure, it's important for Mem and Da to know him and I hope like him, but you have to love him too."

"I think you love him enough for both of us."

"Well I do, in that way, but you've been the most important person in my life forever, so the two of you have to be friends."

"We will be. How could I not like someone who's made you this happy?"

"He does, Kat."

Kat lay in her bed after breaking the connection, reliving the meeting over and over. He had been very nice to her. Bree had obviously told him that she was important to her, which warmed Kat considerably. He hadn't been taken aback by the fact that she was an enforcer, a plus. Even if he were less than thrilled, he'd been able to hide it.

Bree was her sister, in all ways except blood and her happiness necessary to Kat. She would get used to the changes. Look at how much in her life she'd already accustomed herself. At least this change would make her best friend happy.

Chapter Sixteen

Kat's graduation the next week was full of pomp and circumstance. She missed Da. He would have been proud of her on more than one level, knowing that like him, she made the best of what faced her and done a good job. Of course, Gramma Lil's pride nearly overwhelmed her.

Head, wearing his full dress uniform, caused a thrill she felt down to her marrow when he intoned her name, then attached the pin to her lapel. He actually winked at her though she knew no one else had seen it.

She had been stunned after the conferring of pins, to find that she graduated the top of her class. She was aware her marks were good, but still she was stunned. He called her back to the front to award her the certificate. She could hear Gramma Lil, Bree and Danl's clapping above all the others.

It looked as though Head wanted to clap as much as they did. Regardless of her preferences, she would be happy to report to this man.

At the reception following the ceremony, it felt as though everyone in the class came up and spoke to her, congratulating her. She wasn't completely sure all of the comments were sincere, but it felt good, if a little embarrassing, to be the center of attention. Head stood beside her showing what felt like fatherly pride and letting everyone know how he felt about her achievements.

When things finally began to thin out, he turned to her. "I know your traditional education is completed, but I'd like to offer you a position reporting to me for the next cycle. I would be honored to mentor you."

She blinked her astonishment, then smiled. "Sir, *I* would be honored."

Head nodded. "We'll talk in my office. Now, go have fun with your friends."

"Thank you." She stood there as he walked off and jumped a little when Gramma Lil touched her arm. "Do you believe that?"

"Of course I do, what?" Her gramma smiled up at her.

"Head just asked to mentor me this next cycle. Me!"

"I should thump you on the head," Gramma Lil retorted.

"What?"

"You're surprised! My darling Kitten, don't you have any clue how incredible you are?"

"Gramma— "

"She's right," Bree chimed in from her other side. "Did you not know about the award? You looked thoroughly stunned. I am so proud of you."

"Okay, that's enough of that," Kat hugged Lil and then Bree. Danl winked at her and she grinned. They headed back to Kat's apartment for dinner.

"Do you know where you'll be assigned?" Bree asked as she helped put the food out on the table.

"Not really, though if I'm reporting directly to Head, I'll get to stay here at Centerport. Enforcers in their first real cycle usually work in retail, keeping an eye out for petty thieves. The thought is, if you can get an anti-social person into treatment earlier, they don't become true drains on Puter, and hopefully won't escalate to bigger crimes."

"They're actually sent to psych for readjustment?" Danl asked. "I always thought that was just a tale to scare kids."

Kat shook her head. "It's not widely discussed, but people, healthy people don't feel the need to steal from Puter and it doesn't harm anyone. These people are just," she shrugged, "readjusted. Afterwards they go back to their homes and their jobs and fit in like they're supposed to."

"Fit in," Danl repeated. "I guess that's for the best."

Something about that comment made Kat look over at him, but he had turned away. What he said was correct. It *was* for the best, but his tone... They dropped the subject as Bree took her seat at the table.

"Come on, Kat *cooked* this and I want to try it."

Kat cut her eyes at her friend, but took her seat at the head of the table. She forgot about the conversation until alone in bed that night.

For some reason she couldn't get those words out of her head? "Fit in, I guess that's for the best." Simple words, and there was no special inflection when Danl said them. Why were they rolling around in her mind? It *was* a good thing; if people were healthy, they wouldn't harm the colony. There was no good reason for people to steal food or clothing. They were lucky that Puter's abilities included being able to cure these people.

She lay there trying to recall what her training covered about the psych process. It did seem odd that in all those cycles of training only about a day and half were dedicated to that whole area. Her class had visited the facility once. She remembered expecting to see something like a doctor's office, where the doctor and the patient would discuss the problem, get counseling. It had been nothing like that. The facility reminded her more of operating theaters that Gramma Lil had shown her cycles before. Totally sterile, holding only a bed with five point restraints, the starkness was extreme.

There hadn't even been a chair for a doctor to sit with the patient during the process. No recourse or appeal was available for any of it. If you were caught, you were sent to psych regardless of the crime. There were no holding areas, cells to lock people up, because that was never necessary. The same penalty held true from something petty like shoplifting to actual shirking.

That meant the "psych" consisted only of drugs from Puter. Why had she never thought about that before? She, of all people, should have raised questions about the process, but she couldn't remember a single question being asked.

No choice, once again Puter made all of the decisions and his word was more than law.

Their instructor had given them a short presentation at the site. No doctor or attendant joined them and no one ever addressed the class about the issue. She distinctly remembered going to the facility, now that she thought about it, but she couldn't remember clearly what the class did that afternoon. She didn't think they stayed that long. There was certainly nothing to see. As she thought about it, she remembered every one of them had been instructed to log in individually. Usually when they went on site for a demonstration, the instructor or someone in the front of the class used their gimp then everyone else would file in. Not at the psych location, all of the students were been ordered to press their gimp to the reader individually. She remembered it as annoying and more time consuming than she thought necessary.

Embarrassed now, she wondered why she hadn't given this more thought? Danl certainly picked up on it instantly, or he'd given it a great deal of thought before. She needed to give it more thought herself.

Chapter Seventeen

Kat pulled the skirt of the dress up so she could walk faster. She wasn't late, but she had wanted to be early. She wanted to help keep Bree calm. Her friend had shown some nerves, not anxious and absolutely not uncertain, but wanting to make sure that everything went perfectly. Bree and Krystal had spent nearly full time on this ceremony for weeks.

Okay, Kat knew that was a little bit of an exaggeration, but not much. Bree was so happy, no way would Kat bring her down. Fratz, wasn't she wearing this dress! She smiled to herself. She would never wear this kind of outfit for anyone but Bree.

Watching Bree and Danl together still amused and puzzled her, but Bree's happiness delighted her. She had always known that Bree would find someone and contract. They'd known since they were ten cycles old that Bree would reproduce, but Kat still wasn't prepared for the depth of the relationship Bree had developed with Danl. It had taken someone from one of the other arcologies transferring in to get Bree off the available list. She hadn't looked back since Danl had entered her life.

Kat could admit, at least to herself, that she didn't understand it. Maybe Puter had been right about that at least, her not mating or having children. The sex that she experienced, she couldn't say enjoyed, had been embarrassing and... messy more than anything else. Bree confided to her that Danl was the best lover she'd ever known. Kat hadn't had the nerve to ask what that entailed and avoided the whole subject as much as possible. She had the impression that Bree just thought she was being discreet and Kat had seen no reason to disabuse her of that notion.

There hadn't been a lot of time alone with Danl, but she had enjoyed several meals with the two of them. He was smart and funny, and genuinely seemed to like her. He had readily accepted her as part of Bree's family and called her himself to include her on a couple of occasions. He finally admitted to her that the fact that she was an enforcer surprised him. Without dwelling on it, he admitted to her that Bree had told him the story of her training. He hadn't shown her sympathy exactly, but let her know he understood. That was above and beyond, so it warmed her that he included her in his life as well.

Krystal opened the door for Kat and smiled. "Goodness! You look lovely, Kat. Turn around; let me see. That dress is perfect for you."

Kat smiled, even if she didn't believe it. "Bree picked it out."

"And you listened to her. Wise decision," Krystal grinned, giving Kat the once over again. The dress was a long flowing gray silver sheath that flared below the knee and accentuated Kat's lean musculature. The neckline showed off her long graceful neck and even seemed to enhance her cleavage—that is, it gave her some. Kat hadn't discovered what trick caused that, but she did feel, well, almost pretty. Her last "lover" had mentioned her lack of curves. In her uniform, that was unimportant and she never dressed like this. It was a dress-up day and she could pretend, but only for Bree's sake.

Her hair was down today, and as per Bree's instructions curled and bouncy. She looked up when Bree entered the room. Bree was wearing her signature pink, but the lightest shade Kat had ever seen, it was almost a blush. This dress was form fitting and seemed to hint at a deep cleavage, but was actually quite modest. She had sheer long sleeves and that same sheer fabric overlaid her full skirt. Her hair was partially up, curls cascading down her back.

"Oh Kat, that dress turned out even better than I dreamed!" She hurried to her friend, checking her out with a practiced eye.

"Me? Have you looked in the mirror?"

Bree laughed, knowing she did indeed look beautiful today. "I wear feminine clothes all the time. This is different for you, more feminine but even in this you still have that warrior woman look. I should have gotten you a shield—"

"Oh and a sword, please," Kat laughed, twirling slightly to get the full effect of the skirt as it swirled around her feet.

"No, not today. I want *some* of the people to be looking at me."

"Danl hasn't seen anyone else since he met you," Kat reminded her. "Is everything set up in your apartment?"

"Yes," Bree brushed an imaginary flaw from her own skirt. "He stayed there last night."

"I should have made a big 'Do Not Disturb' sign for your door," Kat teased.

"We don't plan to be 'disturbed' even if Puter comes to the door personally," Bree retorted laughing. Kat laughed with her, but secretly shook her head. Maybe someday she would "get" what excited Bree so much about the activity, but now wasn't the time to dwell on it.

Being careful of her dress, she and Krystal gathered up the last minute items needed, combs, pins, and the "list," then went to meet Chark at the large room he had scheduled for a formal contracting ceremony.

They received a lot of stares and smiles as they made their way to the gathering room. What Kat failed to notice was that she received as many appreciative looks as Bree. Krystal saw it and smiled. She wasn't Kat's mother, but had spent a lot of time with her growing up. She knew how thrilled she would be if both of "her" girls found the happiness that Bree had.

The actual ceremony was short and Kat couldn't help being amused at the "hit over the head" look on Danl's face when he spotted Bree. Having that look turned towards her might be nice someday, but she no longer expected or especially wanted it. Why did the image of the young enforcer talking to Head at the graduation last cycle come to her? She shook it off, today was special. What did Gramma called it? A "fairy tale" type day. Reality didn't have a place. She would just enjoy herself.

The celebration following the ceremony was actually fun. A dinner for the attendees had been planned. While Krystal hadn't cooked, Kat could see her hand in the preparation. Wine for toasting, then dancing to celebrate—the perfect celebration. Danl's friend Evan from Secondport stood with him as she stood with Bree, so he became her partner for the dinner and dance. Friendly and a good dancer, better than she was anyway, she found herself really enjoying the party. He seemed interested in her, but she didn't encourage it. She was busy today, making sure that everything went smoothly for Bree and in any case, he would be headed back to Secondport tomorrow.

It was a beautiful day, and she shared a smile with Gramma Lil as Bree and Danl made their way out of the gathering room and on to their new lives together. If Lil's smile was a little wistful, Kat understood and laughed as Evan pulled her back onto the dance floor.

Chapter Eighteen

Davd shut the door firmly behind him and dumped his pack on the bed. It had been a good trip, but he needed to shower and to check in before anyone realized how long he'd been gone.

He was good at that now, but he had to remain cautious. It had been genius to volunteer for gimp liaison. No one wanted the tedious job, therefore no one was checking on him when he was out of communication for short periods. No one knew.

Out of the shower, he checked his pad for any meetings that might have been called while he was gone. No meetings, but a date with Kala tonight. He probably should have gotten out of it, but too late now. She was authorized to have a son and since her graduation, she'd been set on using his DNA for the job.

Wasn't going to happen. She was okay in bed, but he had no plans to contract, therefore no plans to procreate. He'd seen what it did to kids. Fratz, he'd lived it. No way would he put some child through that on purpose. Puter wouldn't miss one male child.

A quick liaison tonight would take the edge off though. Kala was enthusiastic and knowledgeable. She should be with all the practice she got. It didn't matter to him; she was merely a sex partner, no strings. But sometime it might be nice to feel something for the women he slept with, maybe. He knew something was missing at least. Maybe someday the perfect woman would fall into his arms. He laughed to himself as he hurried out.

He made it to roll call early and caught up on what gossip he missed over the last four days. He did marvel at the thick-headedness of his fellow enforcers. They honestly thought the shirkers they brought in, the petty thieves they caught, were the extent of what was going on. They *trusted* Puter. Oh well, it made his job easier. Especially now that Cal was in charge.

He took his assignment and made certain his absence had caused no stir. Alone, he headed out to check on a report of a possible shirker making a nest in a seldom-used area on the factory level.

This was what he was trained for, officially, but no longer his real work. He'd been... stunned wasn't a strong enough word for how he'd reacted when Ralt had approached him. *Ralt* of all people, the man who seemed the epitome of a true rule follower. Shirkers, real shirkers, were among them. There were *villages* on the planet, near each of the arcologies and an underground existed that kept people in contact and informed. They even helped people escape to outside. That no longer felt like a negative word to him. His father had felt that way, though they had never discussed it. Davd regretted that now.

The villages were generations old and those people lived in harmony with the land, not ignoring it or taking it for granted like the box dwellers did.

Having been to the village closest to Thirdport on numerous trips now, helping true escapees and taking in occasional supplies from stasis area—those originally meant for that purpose—he felt at home there. Much more at home than he did here.

A smile grew on his face. He had a home there now. Not big, just for him since he had no plans for a family, regardless of Puter's edict. This was a house he had worked on each trip outside. Now it was there and ready for him when he decided to remain there. Carla had presented him with cushions she had made herself from bright fabric scraps for the chair and couch. The homemade quill that covered his bed had been a present from the community, which had truly humbled him.

****

It had been Ralt who approached him. No one else would have gotten a chance to finish the request. He was a trained enforcer and constantly on the lookout for people trying to go against Puter's edicts. Ralt was barely able to finish and even then Davd though it was a test.

"You *want* me to go outside?" They had been in the garden area of the roof of Thirdport.

"Yes, for short periods of time. I'll take you the first time. I can make arrangements for tomorrow. Your co-workers will just see you take a few days off with family. I know it's a leap of faith, but this is something your grandda and I worked on together. It's important."

"Grandda knew about this?"

Ralt nodded. "He helped set up the conduits. This is no fly by night operation, Davd. Now you're really joining the family business."

Ralt had been right. This was what he was made to do. His training as an enforcer gave him the extra skills to hide the activity and protect others doing the same.

That first trip, riding an honest to Galt *horse*, had not only been eye opening, it had changed his life forever. Someday he wanted to see the other villages. They were newer than Thirdport and had used the hard won knowledge from that endeavor for the planning and setup.

Davd hadn't discussed it with Ralt, but his dream was to lead an expedition to the other villages, over land. They had aerial maps from the original drone survey, but the real experience was important for him and future generations. A village between Thirdport and Centerport, leading to even more for easier access was his goal.

Hadn't there been explorers on Rth that had done this and were still remembered all of these generations later? Lou and Clark? Something like that. Now that was a fine long-term goal.

Chapter Nineteen

Kat watched the short man closely. She knew he was stealing, but catching him wasn't as easy as she had thought it would be. It angered her when people stole, as if it was a personal act against her. She'd pretty much set aside her problems with the psych process. It was necessary to maintain the kind of control needed in such a close environment. There was no *need* to steal here. Everyone was supplied with a home and food. Anyone could work for the little extras they wanted. If someone wanted something more, all they had to do was work a few extra hours. This man looked like he was spending all of his extras on alco-drinks.

The past cycle had been eye opening for her. Of course, what she had learned in class was important, but what Head taught her was even more so. She studied shirkers. That seemed to be an area that was important to Head. There had been little in the curriculum about shirkers. Oh, they had been discussed, but as her instructor was more than fond of saying, "if you did your job correctly..." For the most part, shirkers wanted to get out of their responsibility to Puter. It wasn't just taking things from retail, which of course shirkers did, it was the fact that they refused to interact with others, share ideas and ways to make the colony more efficient. People that shirked were anti-social and that was wrong. It was okay to be private, but to escape to a little known area of the arcology, build a *nest* and live all alone without any contact with Puter was sick.

She'd helped in the capture of several of shirkers now and brought in a couple on her own. Her knowledge of those little explored areas of the arcology turned out to be important after all. She planned to explore that part of the curriculum with Head in one of their debriefings.

Of course, her personal life changed as well. Bree's contract with Danl had been a highlight. The young couple had lost no time conceiving Drew. When he was born, Kat was stunned to watch, as they grew even happier together.

She was moving closer to the man she was following when her com vibrated. She walked quickly away from the crowd and around a corner to keep from tipping him off that he was being observed. When alone, she brought the com to her ear. "43035KPS"

"Head needs to see you right away. I show you in Market 6. How quickly can you be here?"

"I can be there in ten. What I'm on can wait." She slipped the com back in her packet. She would know this man on sight now, so she could continue later. She headed away from the mover. It would be faster walking this time of day.

She made it there in eight and hurried to the administrative area. "Head's looking for me?" Kat stepped into the outer office.

"Yes, go on in. He's in a hurry." His admin pinged Head to let him know that Kat was on her way in.

****

Head leaned back, studying his office as he waited for Kat to enter. Puter's choice about his profession as Head of all enforcers had worked out perfectly. He even enhanced his role of warrior with his appearance, using the pictures he'd studied in class of the old Injuns of Rth. His hair wasn't as dark, more a light brown, but he wore it long and tied back at his neck with a piece of leather. He was tall, even for a colonist at over 1.83 meters, with wide shoulders. He knew he had the look of strength and confidence. He'd used that on more than one occasion in his career. He was younger than he looked, but he'd held his position of authority with the enforcers for cycles.

His office matched him well. Most offices were decorated with regulation walls and screens, but he had worked on this room himself. One wall was actually covered with wood and the hide of an animal was preserved and stretched out on the wall over the seats. He was well aware that everyone assumed it was an animal from Rth, something that his parents thought to bring with them. He did not abuse anyone of that notion.

He turned as Kat entered and watched her admire the trophy. He assessed her silently. She was strong, fairly tall for a woman here on New Home, nearly 1.75 meters. Her pedigree was of the finest; third generation here, with strong genes from Rth. She wore her blonde hair long, pulled back in a braid, perfectly regulation. Her green eyes were steady and calm. She exuded strength and confidence.

He'd watched her since before she came under his supervision, helped her when her da was killed so suddenly. She didn't socialize with many enforcers. He found that he approved of that. Some enforcers needed that interaction to function at their best. That wasn't true of her. She spent more time with her family and her oldest friends and she was the better for it.

He motioned for her to move to his desk. She was agile, moving like the animal of her name and was probably the best enforcer he supervised. Kat used her abilities to see beyond the job into aspects that most enforcers either didn't realize were important or discounted. It made her superior and kept her in Head's sights. Besides, he liked the woman, respected her. She stood in front of his desk, her back straight, her hands clasped behind her. The uniform fit her perfectly, high-waist pants in light gray with a light blue stripe up the legs that matched the sweater. The short jacket partially covered the utility belt she wore, which held her packet containing her discs, ID and backup weapon. Her primary weapon was inside the jacket under her left arm where she could take hold of it easily. The small light blue stripes at her shoulders reminded him of epaulets from older uniforms in pictures he had seen from Rth.

She was one of the reasons they had colonized here; her and others like her—intelligent, healthy, someone to carry on the human race with dignity.

But not her.

He knew that Puter had determined she wasn't to breed. That seemed to be happening more and more with each class as they were assigned their training. Puter decided the optimum population and apparently they had reached it. Only replacements were needed. People normally lived to be around seventy here, their health, their genes superior. Not as long as on Rth, but the gravity here was slightly higher. At least that was what he'd been taught in school. Head was in no position to contradict it. Puter, theoretically, had more information than he did. Puter ran things; that was the way everyone wanted it.

It wasn't his place to question why genes that had been so superior on Rth were so watered down after such a short period that they were destined to be lost from the planet.

Head looked her up and down, then nodded to himself. This was the right decision. "I'm lending you to Thirdport."

****

She blinked, startled at those words, but didn't speak.

"It's a short term assignment. They have a shirker. I know you'll be able to assist them."

"A shirker? Thirdport needs extra personnel to catch a single shirker?" She wasn't really questioning Head, but that sounded odd.

"This shirker is an enforcer."

Kat's mouth dropped open for an instant, then she was back in control. Enforcers didn't shirk; they were the ones that *caught* shirkers. "I see. When do I leave?"

"I'll ensure the shuttle waits for you. Pack for a couple of days at least. Kat, you won't be able to take him physically. He's bigger than you are and he doesn't want to be found. You're as smart as he is. You're going to have to use that to find him."

"Yes, sir."

He handed her a disc and she slipped it into her packet.

She turned and left the office without another word.

****

Head watched until the door closed. He'd made the right decision and for some reason it felt as though time was short. He took a deep breath and forced his attention back to the desk.

There were a lot of details to clean up.

Chapter Twenty

Kat packed quickly. There would be accommodations at Thirdport if she needed to stay. Since it was another enforcer... just the thought caused her to pause again. Yes, she would probably have to stay. Her exercise uniform, she could wear that and pack a spare uniform. Crawling around in the bowels of the arcology might require some athleticism. She could wear her uniform jacket with either. If she needed more, she could requisition some at Thirdport. Her large pack already had her normal supplies, which should be enough.

She reached the port on the roof quickly. It would be a short trip, but the shuttle was often full this time of day. She would have a seat regardless, but disliked having to bump anyone. It wasn't good for the relationship between enforcers and the rest of the population.

She'd never had a problem, but knew of other enforcers who used their clout and position with too heavy a hand. It reflected badly on all of them, but the troublemakers obviously didn't care. Maybe that was one of the reasons they enjoyed the work as much as they did—knowing they could wield power over others. It was her job and as with everything, she did her very best. The thought came unbidden—as she would have as a doctor. Shoving that aside for the billionth time, she approached the shuttle loading area.

Luckily, there were several empty seats, so no one was inconvenienced by her sudden appearance. She gazed out, her eyes unfocused as the different shades of green slipped under her. She forgot, as so many of the colonists did, how unexplored and wild the countryside surrounding Centerport was. The forests, actually jungles as they were in this direction, were thick and impenetrable. Puter was careful not to harm the native areas, even between the three ports. The only way to visit between the three arcologies was air travel of course, as no roads had ever been constructed.

No one ever went outside.

That brought her back to her assignment with a jolt. Most shirkers only disappeared into the unoccupied places within the arcologies. They hid in the deep mechanical areas of the structures, stealing what they needed from the vendors just above them. It was their way of avoiding responsibility to themselves, their families and Puter. Obvious mental health issues were involved and once caught—and so far she brought back every one assigned—were placed in the hospital until their psychosis was healed, then eventually returned to society. She'd only heard legends of shirkers successfully getting "outside" since she started her training. The thought had never occurred to her before her training. Those people were never seen again, probably starved to death. It did happen though, somehow. It was never mentioned officially, but every shirker was *not* caught. That was an issue not taught in the training. Working with Head had brought that factoid to her attention.

She'd never asked Head about the legends and now she wondered how she could have skipped such an obvious topic.

An Enforcer shirker would know. This enforcer she was hunting would have her same training, maybe some similar experiences. Would such a shirker go "outside?" No one could survive out there, no food, no shelter, not even any clean water. She couldn't understand why anyone would want to take such a risk. Puter provided everything anyone needed; you had only to do your own work and receive the benefit of ages of technology from Rth and New Home. What would make someone so unhappy that they would attempt such a dangerous path?

She opened her packet and without thought let her finger rub over an older disc, the oldest in her packet. She'd taken it from Gramma Lil cycles ago. She knew now that Gramma had known, but she hadn't reported her. No one, except maybe Bree, knew how much she'd studied it and still checked it on occasion. Basic medical information didn't really change.

She shook that off and slipped this newest disc from Head into her reader.

A shirker. She didn't understand why she had been tapped for this assignment, but she didn't question Head any more than she would Puter. She leaned back. Why run? What was the motivation? They had everything they needed in the arcologies. Puter made sure of that and there was no emotion to cloud his judgment. How many times had she heard that? Puter determined she should be an enforcer.

Now Head thought she could bring in an enforcer shirker.

That caused a slight smile to her face. She *was* good, even if it wasn't her choice. She looked back down at the reader and let it run.

She didn't know the man in the picture, but there was something familiar about him. She knew many enforcers, through training and working in the field, but not this one. He had dark hair and eyes and stood a little over 1.8 meters with an excellent build. 41219DGP, Davd Palfy, two cycles older than her. He would be considered hot by every female on the planet, if even his official picture was this good. Missing two days and they were just now realizing it? Fratz! That was going to make it harder. Most shirkers—no forget that, this man wasn't most shirkers. An enforcer... he actually could be out of the arcology by now, which meant a trip outside.

She'd never been outside. She'd never had to go. If you did your work correctly... Head thought she could do it, and she would never let him down. But first she would have to ensure the man wasn't hidden somewhere in the deep infrastructure. That could take awhile. With a sigh, she settled back to rest. Who knew when she'd get her next real sleep.

Shoving thoughts of the chase to come out of her mind, she relaxed her muscles as she had been taught.

Chapter Twenty-One

Thirdport was newer than Centerport with some slight differences in technology since it was the last transport from Rth. This had all happened long before her birth, but was still discussed as though the next contact would be any day.

She confirmed her arrival to Puter, obtaining directions to enforcer headquarters. She needed more information on this Davd; more than just the specs from Puter. She needed to talk to people who knew him, see where he lived, and find out what his motive for shirking might be.

Head of the enforcers here at Thirdport, known as Cal rather than his title, since Head was the true head of all of the enforcers, was a lot younger than Head at Centerport, and with a lot less presence or authority. He seemed grateful for her assistance in what he referred to as an "embarrassing matter."

Well that was probably true. She couldn't remember even hearing about an enforcer shirking. Usually it was people that couldn't fit in. Enforcers were screened for that kind of thing. They respected authority; they understood the rules and accepted Puter's decisions without question.

She grimaced internally at that. Okay, somewhere deep inside of her, it still rankled, but whatever her assignment it was for the best, for the good of everyone here. Maybe it wasn't buried that deep inside of her, but it was a fact and she lived with it.

"I'm going to need access to 41219DGP's gimp, his apartment and his latest transmissions. Do you have—"

"His gimp isn't transmitting." This obviously was difficult for the supervisor, Cal, to say and Kat looked at him for a long moment.

When he said nothing further, she asked, "When did it stop?"

"We, uh, we don't know. Davd was in charge of monitoring that information for Thirdport."

When Kat didn't respond, the man's face hardened. "He's been an enforcer for cycles. He's one of the best I've ever seen and there was no reason to distrust him."

"You know him well?"

"I thought I did. He's just a couple of cycles younger than I am. We knew each other in school, played sports together."

"He's very athletic?"

"Yes, and skilled at all of the games."

"I might need to talk to his family, other friends."

"I can give you the name of some friends, there is no family."

"No family?"

The supervisor shook his head. "His parents didn't sign for a long term contract. His father moved to Secondport cycles ago. He was killed in a construction accident shortly after that. His mother, well she became a little strange after that. She left him alone a lot. It wasn't a great childhood."

"And Puter still made him an enforcer?" she said that aloud without thinking.

"I don't question Puter," his voice was hard now and she nodded.

"If I could get that list please, and directions to his apartment, I would appreciate it." It obviously rankled that Head himself had sent someone from another port to investigate.

Cal nodded curtly and rose. She did as well and followed him to the outer office. He opened the file himself and fed the information into her gimp. She thanked him and left the office.

She took only a moment to get her bearings, then headed toward the mover that would take her closest to his apartment. She kept her pack on her rather than leave it at headquarters. There was no telling what she would need and having her own pack, meant she was prepared. She felt more sure than ever that she'd have to go outside now. Missing for a couple of days with no record of when he'd deactivated his gimp. Frack! That act alone showed his commitment to shirking. He'd broken all contact with Puter. Okay, the man was a trusted member of the enforcers, but fratz...

She used her gimp to open his apartment. As an enforcer, that authority was hers at all locations. The apartment was small; smaller than her place it seemed and she was in a single herself. No reason to make a formal contract and crowd your life when there would be no children.

Was this Davd authorized to reproduce? She pulled his personal information up again and checked. Yes, one child, male, but there was no contract on file for him either. Not unheard of, but unusual. People that were allowed to reproduce usually did it young and signed at least a short-term contract. Maybe because of his father...

The short-term contracts were more fashionable lately, with fewer and fewer people given the authorization to reproduce. Even those that were authorized no longer seemed to bother with the long term, not like Bree and Danl. She looked around the place. This wouldn't take long to search. She started in the bedroom area. Clothing was missing, but not everything. All of his regulation boots were gone though, she noted. She spotted a frame, lying face down and picked it up.

Empty.

Okay, he'd taken whatever had been housed in it. His family? A woman he was thinking of contracting? There was no way to know without asking one of his friends. The kitchen area was empty; he'd cleaned before he left. What about portable food? Even if he packed some food, it couldn't be enough to sustain him for long.

What was his plan? Had he decided to terminate? A lot of people did that now, more than the public realized. No, why take the boots in that case. But he certainly couldn't have enough supplies to last him outside for any length of time. Was there any way to carry enough supplies for such a thing?

The buzzer of the doorbell startled her and she automatically reached for her stunner. Shaking her head, she moved toward the door. She scanned a young woman waiting just outside.

An olive complexioned woman, with dark, intelligent eyes and long shiny, almost black hair waited for entry. Her hair was artfully arranged around her shoulders. She was in casual clothing, so Kat couldn't tell her profession. Her first thought, catty maybe but accurate, was that she could be a professional sex worker. The clothing certainly fit. Her breasts, which had to have been enhanced—a lot—okay, that was definitely catty, were barely covered by the thin cloth and her navel, adorned with ring, was exposed. The pants were tight, and low cut, to better display her abs. Hell, this woman's exercise routine might make her eligible for enforcer training.

Kat opened the door and the woman started back, obviously surprised to see her.

"Uh, is Davd here?"

"No. Are you a friend of his?"

"We know each other." There was a slight defensiveness to her tone. She wanted to stake her claim, but a fellow enforcer—a woman—was inside his apartment. "We were supposed to meet for, uh, for lunch, but he didn't show. I wanted to make sure he was..."

Kat stepped back to allow her to enter. "He's not here right now. Would you like to leave a message?"

"No. No, thank you." Her voice became a little more formal. She'd taken the time to assess Kat's appearance now and found it lacking. "Is everything all right?"

"Could you tell me what was in this frame?" Kat ignored her question and picked up the empty frame again.

"That was a picture of him and his boss, I think. I've never met the other man. Where is it?"

Kat shook her head. "You say you were supposed to meet him for lunch today? I'm sorry, I missed your name."

"M'gan. Yes, today. Is something wrong?"

"I hope not. If you're going to leave a message..." Kat pointed to the counter where the pad lay.

"No, that's okay. I'll try to catch up with him later." She was already moving toward the door. She opened it and was gone before Kat could decide whether to ask anything else. Didn't matter, she'd be easy enough to find if there was any reason.

The pad, what messages had been left on it? She grabbed it up and fed in the universal code to unlock it. There were several messages, apparently he'd made this decision to run spontaneously, or had left a trail to confuse whoever was given the assignment to catch him. She was beginning to suspect the latter.

An enforcer was trained to make quick decisions in the field, but plan for every contingency ahead of time. These appointments were jumbled, on top of each other. She looked farther back in the history.

At four days ago, there was a short message that made no sense. Until then the messages had been mostly from women. She sniffed at that, he was obviously a popular sex partner. She wondered idly if all of these women were looking for superior genes, or just a roll with a hot male. From the picture on his disc, it could easily be either one.

This message was strange. N12-172-KPS. That was all, no words. KPS, it had to be a coincidence that those were her initials. N12? That didn't mean anything yet. 172... that was three days ago, if they were talking about dates, it was most likely the day he disappeared. So what was N12? And who was the message from? She scanned back and was stunned to realize that the message sender was unobtainable. It had been completely erased from the system. Kat hadn't realized such a thing was even possible. The message must have come from someone with superior coding skills or someone with access to high administration. An ally? This could be bigger than she originally thought.

She'd learned everything she could from his apartment for now. She tucked his pad into her pack and left.

Now she needed to know if he truly was outside, and how.

She wasn't familiar with Thirdport personally, but the design should be basically the same as Centerport. She found an alcove near a food stand and took a seat, pulling out her pack. She pulled up the schematics from Puter.

It took a few minutes to verify her access, but shortly she was scrolling through the plans. As with Centerport, there were no easy access points to outside. According to Gramma Lil, the plan had originally been to branch out from the arcologies into smaller villages close to one of the arcologies as a base. Eventually to populate the entire planet, but that hadn't happened. Even the small villages created during construction were long gone.

Puter was very meticulous about not causing any pollution surrounding the huge structures that housed the humans on the planet, but every once in a while Kat idly wondered why there had been so little expansion.

Regardless, the only access to outside was in the lowest levels of the structure, below retail, even below the facilities area. Those plans were restricted, but she continued to drill down into the information with her access.

She leaned back and rubbed her eyes. She needed a larger screen, but she didn't want to go back to the enforcer headquarters. Instead, she headed toward a food dispenser and chose a quick hand meal so that she could continue her investigation.

She zoomed in again, making at least part of the information readable. There were numbers and letters coming into focus now.

The large entrance used when the settlement was still outside, was centered in her screen now. She'd never realized how many smaller entries were also aligned along the bottom of the structure. It made sense, considering the size of the structure no one would expect everyone to use one mammoth entrance on one side of the structure. These smaller entrances were aligned all along the ground level. Why had she never checked this?

She remembered being surprised when, even in her training as an enforcer, there was no actual visit to the exit. She had been told that Puter was fool proof about getting outside, but a shirker could possibly get into others' apartments or even into the mechanical workings of the arcology. Well, she'd just proven the hole in that theory. Enforcers at least, needed to go to these areas, study them, and really know the areas they were protecting. She was definitely going to bring this up to Head when she got back.

She leaned in, squinting to see since the screen, which was now at maximum.

E4. That was the designation of the entrance closest to the main opening. E4? N, was there an N? She raced her finger over the screen, rotating the picture to the left. Yes, Ns! The entrances on that side of the structure were designated as N. That was a concept Gramma Lil said they had brought from Rth. Something to do with the magnetic fields, what were the words? E for "east", yes.

Was there an N12? 4, 8, yes.

Kat felt adrenaline flood her body. Was this the way he had left the arcology? If so, it was three days ago. And why her initials? That was the part that made the least sense to her. She hadn't been assigned this case until after he left and then by Head himself.

Whatever, checking the site personally was her next step. She slid her screen back into her pack after memorizing the location and wiping it. She grabbed a protein snack and bulb of water then took a seat close to the recycling chute. In Centerport, the recyclers reset every hour. That should be the same here, so she had ten mins to wait.

This Davd wouldn't have left any signs of his escape behind, but she needed to see the area anyway.

When the automatic doors opened, Kat looked around quickly, then slipped in past the cart and into the bowels of the structure. Her uniform gave her access, but no need to advertise. She followed the track of the cart to a maintenance door. She pulled on it and she wasn't really surprised to find it unsecured.

Now what? Even in her own arcology, she had only been below this level a few times, and never below the facilities area. How could they not have seen this hole in her training? Shirkers were rare, petty thievery was much more common. When people had everything they wanted... Were they that discontent with their lives? She remembered people complaining about Puter on occasion, it didn't happen anymore with her, not wearing this uniform. Just how widespread was the discontent?

Fratz! She pushed on, moving downward, making her way toward this N-12 entry. Maybe she should have left her pack at headquarters after all, but she wasn't going to leave it down here. She shrugged it more comfortably on her shoulders and kept moving. There was light, but it wasn't sufficient to see much between the dim globes. Her own small light wasn't helping much either in an area this large. She could see the steps in front of her, but the area beyond that was very large and very dark. This area was off limits to most people, just for occasional inspections. She let her hand lightly brush against the railing, moving a little more swiftly when more light was available.

She knew the structure descended several floors below ground, to house and stabilize the entire infrastructure necessary for such a large area and population. Kat was pleased to find that the stairs were labeled with the level. She trotted down to ground on the metal stairs. No attempt was made to make this area inviting in any way.

She turned to the right and saw a small glow over the nearest door. N8 was stenciled on the metal door. She needed N-12, so she continued to the right. For the first time since she'd entered the area, she spotted some trash on the floor. She bent down and retrieved it. A wrapper to a protein bar, just like the one she had eaten upstairs. They were common enough, but popular with enforcers who often didn't have time for meals.

Would this careful enforcer-trained man have made a mistake, or was he leading her?

She moved closer to the door and was able to read the N-12 on the plaque over the top. Okay, there *was* an N-12. Had this Davd gone out through it three days ago?

Their enforcers should have been able to track this. Did they just not want their people at Thirdport to know about this "embarrassing situation"? That was a better explanation for bringing someone in from Centerport. Now, did she call for back up or check the exit herself?

He already had a three-day head start. She didn't have to track him; she could just look around and see if she could spot anything. Once again, the door was not secured. She took a deep breath and pushed the heavy door open.

The bright light blinded her for an instant and she staggered, then it all went dark.

Chapter Twenty-Two

There was light on the other side of her eyelids, but the pain in her head kept her from wanting to see it. What the flaming frak had happened? She couldn't remember much beyond her name right now.

She started to roll over, but her stomach vehemently protested that movement.

"Take it easy." The voice was deep and reassuring somehow, but who was here with her?

She opened her eyes a bit then, squinting into the light, but she couldn't focus. "Wha—" Nope, too much. Breathing through her mouth seemed to help a little. She wouldn't try that again for now.

"Slow down your breathing. You'll be okay in a couple of minutes."

Again the voice was low and warm and relaxing, which for some reason ticked her off greatly. Who the—oh fratz! It was her target, the man she'd been sent to recover! He hadn't left. He'd gotten behind her. Head had warned her she couldn't take him physically; she'd have to outsmart him. Well that certainly worked out well, she thought, furious with herself.

Her hand came up to her head, checking for blood.

"You're not bleeding."

"Thanks," she said bitterly. "Thanks for pulling your blow."

"I didn't hit you."

Damn his voice was soothing, sexy even, which made her even angrier for some reason. "I ran into a door, right?"

"More through a door, but you can go with that."

She opened her eyes a slit again and glared at him.

"Okay," he grinned. "You're going to be okay. I'm pretty sure you have a hard head."

"Son of a—"

"Hey, let's not get personal here." He sounded a little too amused.

She forced herself to sit up then. His hand came out to steady her. She jerked away and pain flared again.

"I don't want to hurt you," he said.

"Oh yeah, that's damn obvious."

He held his hands up in surrender. "You're not going to believe me anyway, but I did not strike you or harm you in any way. Have you never taken one of the small doors before?"

"I've never tried to shirk, no."

"Never chased someone out before?"

"We catch them before they get that far," she retorted with some spirit now that her anger was feeding her.

He chuckled, not at all offended. "So you don't know about the fail safes. Take it easy, I wouldn't try to move around too much right now."

"Fail safes?" What was he talking about?

"Puter doesn't want anything getting in or out, so there's a failsafe when the door is opened. It's a major jolt, and usually a damn good deterrent. I'm not kidding; you should just sit for a few minutes."

She didn't want to take his advice, but he was right. If she didn't want to lose that last meal, she needed to take it. Already thinking as an enforcer, when would she get her next meal? Cautiously she turned her head and saw the canopy of green above her.

Her eyes widened. "Where the frak are we?" she demanded. Her head still ached, though she didn't think she'd disgrace herself now. When she'd opened her eyes to light, she had assumed they were inside. Holy fratz!

"Well, since I'm officially a 'shirker' now, I guess you are too. You are what is known as 'outside'."

Outside? No, that wasn't... Her heart rate quickened and her head swiveled, taking in the sight, the pain of the movement lost in the adrenaline rush. There was no sign of Thirdport. She jerked her head back toward him. "No!"

"Just relax, it's not that bad."

"Not bad? You can't just kidnap me."

"Hey, you were the one following me," he reminded her. "I was fine on my own."

She glared at him. "You were shirking. It's my job, *our* job if you recall, to keep people from leaving the arcologies. Puter has determined—"

"We need to set up for the night," he cut her off.

"We're not staying out here all night?"

"Actually several nights."

Her face went slack from shock. He looked serious. They were actually going to stay outside overnight?

Davd looked away then. "I'll set up a tent for us."

"Tent? Where are we?"

"Outside of the box, as it were." He rose then and moved behind her. She turned carefully, now leery of the pain in her head again. She jerked back, startled at the sight. There were three large animals tied up behind her. Two of them were eating the foliage near the ground, the third was watching her.

"What the frak are those?" She scooted back a little farther from them.

"Horses."

She goggled at him. "Horses? Real horses?"

"Do they look fake?"

Her eyes narrowed again. "Where did they come from?"

"They were with the stored embryos that Rth sent with us."

"You thawed horses?"

"Not personally, no."

She sputtered for a moment, then turned away from him. This added a new dimension to the problem. This was beyond definite proof he had help. Someone had assisted him to run and given him "transportation."

If she could get loose, she would head back to Thirdport. They couldn't be that far away. He could stay out here to rot for all she cared. What an arrogant son of a bitch.

She watched out of the corner of her eyes as he set up a tent. When he approached her, he held out his hand to help her to her feet.

She ignored it. "You can't keep me out here."

"You want to walk back? Do you know which way? I'm not giving you one of the horses."

She glanced again at the large animals. "I rode—"

"Well, yes and no. You were more slung over the horse in front of me." The look of outrage on her face seemed to amuse him. "I always thought of myself as a breast man, but after watching that ass for hours, I may have converted."

She reached up to slap him, but he caught her wrist. "Just being honest, ma'am. And, since I don't think it would be a good idea for you to try to escape in the night, I'm going to tie you up. I don't want to hurt you, but I have to keep you safe as well."

"Gee, you're a real stand up kind of guy, aren't you?" Her voice was hostile.

For some reason that seemed to bother him, but he made no comment, continuing with set up.

The phrase registered with her then. Hours? She'd already been outside for hours? She spotted the small, flesh-colored bandage on her wrist then and gasped. "My gimp? You didn't!"

Davd didn't meet her eyes.

"You removed my gimp?" Her outrage was tempered with fear now.

"Sorry, necessary." He held up his own wrist and she saw that his gimp was also removed.

"Necessary? We can't stay out here. We can't live out here. There are wild animals, the water isn't clean. What will we eat?"

"Isn't that why we came here? Why our ancestors traveled over light cycles at terrible risk to themselves? To live on this planet, to build a civilization and spread out over the whole world?" He sounded angry now. "But Puter has made a unilateral decision to keep us all boxed up. We're not colonizing anything. We're stagnating. Our population isn't going up, it's exactly even. Puter thinks we have enough people or maybe it's all he can control. He certainly isn't explaining anything to me."

She had leaned back, away from him. His passion had erupted without warning.

He saw her movement and took a deep breath. "You'll be fine without the gimp."

"And you know this because? How many other people have you kidnapped and brought out here?"

He gave her a grim smile. "Don't worry about it."

"I understand you don't want to be tracked, but the gimp also keeps us healthy. It controls hormone levels, vitamins, everything."

"You've absorbed enough to keep you healthy for a long time."

She didn't respond, just staring at him. He sighed, then returned to his work.

She looked back at the small bandage on her arm. She'd never been without her gimp. Since she was an infant it had been there, like her eyelashes or her lungs. She knew it kept her safe and healthy. Now, as an enforcer, she relied on it for all kinds of information to do her work. It had never occurred to her that she would be without that connection.

With the tent up, Davd pulled some prepared meals out of the pack and pressed on the lids to heat them. They ate in silence, then he pointed to a bush just out of the clearing.

"I'll wait here, you can use that."

She just stared at him for a long moment. "Are you kidding?"

"I don't travel with a luxury bath ensemble. You can try to hold it for several days," he offered unhelpfully.

She shot him a look that should have singed his hair, then rose with dignity and disappeared behind the bush.

****

He watched her go. She wasn't the type of woman that usually captured his time. He liked his companions slightly less headstrong. Still she'd been chosen for some reason. He would no doubt be informed when he needed the information. There were a lot of things about this mission that could use more explanation.

She was wearing the exercise uniform of an enforcer, better for tracking in the bowels of the arcology and looked the worst for wear right now, after her encounter with the failsafe and lying over his saddle for a couple of hours. He'd worn the same uniform since graduation. Of course, she looked better in it than he did. Even after what she'd gone through, all she really needed was to re-braid her hair and she'd be okay to report to Head.

He'd checked her pack while she was out. She had packed light, her regular uniform and what she was wearing. Bet she looked hot in that as well. He didn't recognize some of the stuff she was carrying, but it didn't matter.

Maybe not his type, but he hadn't been kidding about that ass of hers. It was firm and tight. It was obvious she took her training seriously. Her breasts were firm and high, not overly large—which had become the style lately. She certainly looked feminine, but not enough to get in the way when she drew her weapon. In fact, he was sure that she'd had no bodywork done at all. She was the real thing. Her legs were long and strong, her torso lean and toned. She kept herself in excellent shape. He'd seen that when the failsafe hit her. She hadn't gone down immediately, taking two blasts. Hell, he'd gone down after one himself the first time.

Yes, he could definitely see what they saw in her. They needed people like her.

When she returned, he had restraints out.

"Were you serious about restraining me? Where do you think I could go in the dark?"

"It's a safety precaution for me. You're an enforcer. I'm an enforcer. Wouldn't you do the same?"

She didn't bother to answer, extending her wrists and glaring at him. He hoped she didn't notice the twinkle in his eye.

Chapter Twenty-Three

The horses were restless, skittish and it was harder to stay seated today, especially with her meager experience. It was a good thing he had finally decided to untie her hands for travel this morning.

She slept better last night than the night before. There was really no choice, sheer exhaustion could make for good sleep. The only problem was she awoke pressed up against him. Yes, she'd been warmer, but she was an enforcer, she should be able to withstand a little cold.

And no, she wasn't going to admit it felt good, or that she was admiring his damn body even more as he rode ahead of her. Bree would do that, not her.

Bree, would she ever see her again, or Gramma?

She needed to kick herself, she wasn't paying the attention she should so that she could escape and find her way home.

She tightened her grip on the reins with one hand and the saddle with the other instinctively, just as her horse reared. An animal, a large feline, sprang out of the tall grass without warning and attacked the horse she rode. It reared again, screaming, and she felt Davd's arms pulling her free of her horse. He shoved her behind him, even as her feet were touching the ground. How had he dismounted so quickly? She no idea how she managed to keep her balance. His weapon was in his hand that fast and he fired. Her horse was down now, its right front leg hanging by a thread.

The cat turned toward the source of its pain and leapt again. The swipe of its claws caught Davd's jacket as he was going down. Fortunately, she was standing far enough behind him not to go down with him as he fell. She wrenched his weapon from his hand as he landed and automatically thumbed the setting to maximum. She fired as the cat reared back to make a second attack. It looked up at her as though in astonishment before it sank to the ground, finished. The whole thing couldn't have taken more than fifteen secs.

Were there more of them? Did these things travel in packs? Breathing heavily she looked down at Davd. Blood, a lot of blood was coming from his shoulder. The jacket hadn't protected him enough.

If there was another one of those things, she was dead, they all were.

Why the bloody fratz had these things not been studied when they arrived on the planet? Why had she never heard of this kind of animal, even seen a picture? They were living on *its* planet. Frig it; she needed to check on him. She dropped to her knees beside him and gingerly pulled the jacket from his wound. No arterial spray, but that only meant he would bleed to death a little slower. The bleeding had to be stopped now. Where was her pack?

She rose and turned immediately to the packhorse. Its eyes were still white all around.

Quivering, it allowed her to approach with her hand out. She'd never hurt it and the horse had seen her kill the menace. At least it wasn't racing away.

She opened the bundle and spotted the strap of her pack. She yanked it free and pulled it open. Her pack was different from most enforcers, thanks to Gramma Lil, and she dug in, finding the clotter immediately.

Using the cutter in her kit, she quickly sliced away the remains of his jacket and shirt. She gently placed the clotter over the wound and carefully spread the putty-like substance over the entire area. If the wound wasn't too deep, it would stop the bleeding and get some antibiotics into his system. Gramma Lil swore by it. When the wound was completely covered, she drew a deep breath. Had she gotten it on in time?

Second priority was the remaining two horses. She was lucky they hadn't bolted, but she needed to make sure they stayed with them now. There were no trees close enough to suit her, so she shoved a stake into the ground and wrapped the reins of both horses around it. She could come up with something better in a little while.

With the horses steadier, she began unloading the packhorse. She got the tent out and with only a couple of false starts, was able to set it up. Davd needed to be inside somewhere and warm, to try to keep shock down. Her choices were limited.

Once the tent was up, she turned back to him. Good thing he was still unconscious, because she was going to have to drag him, and that would have hurt. A lot.

It took a while, he was definitely not fat, but very muscular and she didn't want to jerk him. She was sweating and out of breath by the time she got him inside. She covered him, to help stave off shock, then sank down beside him just watching for a moment while she got her breath back. She needed to center herself. She still had a lot to do.

He'd saved her life. The SOB had kidnapped her, taken her into the middle of no-fraking-where, nearly gotten her killed, then saved her life.

She took some more deep breaths. Once the shakes were driven away, she returned to check on the horses and scout around, keeping his weapon ready in her hand. There was no sign of any more of those cat things, but then she hadn't seen any sign of the first one, until the claws were swiping at her.

She needed to do something with the carcasses of the cat and the horse. The smell of them might attract other... things.

Kat looked over at the horses; they were still more restless than usual. What did that mean? She took a deep breath and began cooking the animal. It was large, close to the size of the horses, but covered in short fur—a mottled brown with green stripes. What perfect camouflage for this area. It took a while, but she turned it into charcoal. When she was done, she turned to the fallen horse.

That was more difficult somehow. This horse had carried her; its reaction to the cat-thing helped save her life. Did people become attached to these things, like pets? With regret, she also turned the body of the horse into charcoal after removing the saddle. She could only hope that would help keep them safe tonight. It would take awhile for Davd's stunner to recharge, but she'd found her stunner in her pack, so they should be okay. Well, as okay as they could be out here.

She shook her head and turned to the supplies. She needed to eat and he would need water when he woke. She refused to allow herself to dwell on never going back, never seeing Gramma Lil or Bree again.

She chose a meal from the pack and pressed the top to heat it. Should she have a fire tonight? Would a fire keep whatever those things were away? Could she keep a fire under control? Davd was obviously more familiar with this area, but he was in no shape to help. She fed the horses, ensured they were unable to wander off, and returned to the tent.

He was still unconscious, but the clotter was supple and moist, so it was still working.

Exhausted, she decided to stretch out for a little while. She needed to keep him warm and her body needed rest. That was a tenet every enforcer lived by. Any noise would wake her; she knew that.

Kat removed her jacket, tacky with his blood now. She made herself comfortable, lying close to his uninjured side. She forced her mind to clear. She knew she needed to conserve her strength for the long haul.

Chapter Twenty-Four

She woke a couple of times during the night due to his restless movements. He had called out for "Ralt" to help him once and mumbled other things she hadn't understood, but there was no fever and the clotter was still working. There wasn't a whole lot else she could do out here. He was still unconscious, but that was partially from the clotter. Hopefully he wasn't getting worse.

She woke at dawn to find Davd had moved closer to her, or she'd moved closer to him, and her arm was over his chest as she lay facing him, her face nestled into his uninjured shoulder. It felt good and somehow safe.

Kat blinked and moved away quickly. That wasn't like her; she'd never shared a bed all night with anyone. And this man wasn't someone who should make her feel safe. The movement woke him and he turned to look at her. He started to sit up and fell back with a gasp of pain.

"Take it easy," she said quickly. "Don't move around too much."

"Wha—"

"What happened? One of your pets out here in the wild attacked us."

He looked puzzled. "I don't..."

"Some kind of cat, a large one, brown and green? It attacked out of the brush. It killed my horse and nearly killed you."

His eyes widened and he looked down at his shoulder. "You saved me?" Was he incredulous that she'd been able to, or that she'd bothered?

"It was kind of a mutual effort. You pulled me off my horse as it was going down. You managed to fire at the thing, but it swiped you. I grabbed your weapon and killed it."

Davd blanched. "You killed a 'liger' with a stunner?"

"Liger?"

"Lion and tiger. They were large cats back on Rth, we started calling them that."

"Who's we?" she asked instantly. It was the first slip he'd made. There were others out here? She was beginning to suspect more than a few—horses for gault's sake!

"They're dangerous. I can't believe you..."

"There wasn't a lot of choice," she said dryly. "Besides, I've had the same training as you, remember? Do these 'ligers' travel in packs?"

"No, they're single hunters. They have their own territory."

"Well, that's one thing in our favor. Don't suppose you'd be willing to head back to civilization and get that wound looked at?"

He looked at her for a long moment. "What more would they be able to do that you can't?"

She started back. "What?"

"I don't carry this blue stuff in my pack and I'm not sure I'd put it on correctly if I did."

She turned away; she could feel the color in her cheeks. There was nothing wrong with carrying medical supplies in her pack. The fact that she knew how to use them shouldn't embarrass her after all this time. She poured him some water and brought it to his lips. "Here, you're probably dehydrated."

He drank some, watching her. "Thanks." She felt of the clotter. It was hard now, drying. "Is it okay?"

"Yes. Enough medicine is in your system; it's turning into a scab, a bandage now, just for protection."

"I didn't know they did that."

"They usually aren't left on this long. At home, you'd have been taken to a clinic and wouldn't need it. Are you in a lot of pain?"

He thought about it for a moment. "It aches, but not sharp pain."

"Good, there's pain medication in the clotter as well as antibiotics. Looks like I did it right."

"Yeah, it does."

Again, she looked away. "I'll fix you a sling." His eyes seemed to see more than they should when he looked at her. All of this was his fault, she shouldn't think about compliments from him as anything but guilt on his part.

"We should get moving. We've never studied how long it takes for one of the ligers to take over additional territory."

"You're not ready to travel yet. You need to eat to replace the blood you lost."

"I didn't know you cared," he said, his voice sounded low, sexy.

"I don't. But I don't know the way home without you."

"Ahh," he placed his hand over his heart. "You wound me."

"Not as much as the liger did."

He chuckled then and she felt it in the pit of her stomach. Why the frak was she remembering how it felt to wake cuddled up against him? He wasn't a sex partner, he wasn't even a friend. She forced herself back to the present.

"I'll fix you something light to eat, then feed the horses."

"The other two, they're okay?" he asked quickly. It looked like he was chastising himself for not thinking of them immediately.

"Yeah, they were shaken, but they didn't run away. I think they were too scared to move."

"They're lucky you were here to protect them," he said, his voice sounded serious now.

She shrugged and moved out of the tent before he could speak again. She hated this man, he had humiliated her, hell, *kidnapped* her. There would have been no need to save her life if he had just left her alone, or not run himself. She had let Head down, she was unable to finish her assignment and her family would soon be frantic if she didn't check in. What would it do to Gramma Lil to lose her too? They and Castra had been each other's only family for so long. Kat tried to turn her thoughts away. How could she manage, knowing she would never see the people she cared about again?

The horses seemed glad to see her. She fed and watered them, and found herself stroking their manes. She was growing fond of them. Something like this would never make up for what she was losing, though. There was a way home, there must be. Resolute again, she grabbed food for the two of them.

Davd was attempting to sit up when she reentered the tent. The color had drained from his face.

"Hey, what are you doing?"

"You were gone a long time. I wanted to check—"

She glared at him. "I can't feed the horses fast enough for you?"

"Apparently not," his voice was a little frosty now.

She felt a moment of regret that she tried to shove away. He was the one to put her in danger, put *them* in danger, she reminded herself. She didn't have to feel anything for him except anger. So why was she concerned about his feelings?

"Lie back. You don't need to pull on that shoulder. I'll fix you something to eat. Just rest."

He watched her, saying nothing, but he finally eased back down. "We can't stay here."

"So you've told me. How do I get you on the horse? And where do I ride?" She didn't look at him as she prepared the food.

"I can still mount a horse. We'll ride together."

She looked up suddenly at that and nearly dropped his breakfast. "To-together?" Ride all day pressed up against him as she'd been this morning? No, that was impossible.

"We still need the pack horse. We won't be too heavy."

"It's not... You can't ride."

"I'll have to. You can handle the reins and I'll hold on to you."

She couldn't control the blush, but turned away. Working with the food, she asked, "How much farther is it?"

"We'll have to travel slower, not overtax the horse. A couple of days."

"Are you going to tell me where we're going?" Any information could help her.

He sighed. "There's a... settlement. We're going there."

"A *settlement*?" She was looking at him now. "You have a village or something out here in the wilderness?"

"It's what we came here to do, isn't it?"

She didn't have an immediate answer to that.

"Puter," he spat the word.

She blinked and drew back slightly.

"We came here to colonize the planet, the whole damn planet. Instead *Puter* has decided to box us all up in three little squares."

Kat stared at him for a moment. "Puter knows about—"

"Why? Why do you think Puter knows something we don't?"

"Be—because he's *Puter*. The original colonists had him programmed on Rth. They had the information from an entire planet of people—"

"Who never lived here!" he interrupted. "Who knew absolutely nothing about this planet, which is the way Puter wants it to stay."

Her lips moved but no words came.

"Puter didn't exactly do right by you," he declared. "Why the frak are you defending—"

"Hold it! What do you think you know about me?"

He looked abashed at that and turned to his food.

"No." She refused to give up this time. "This is the second time you've gone off on Puter. I get it, you don't like being controlled. But what do you mean—Puter didn't do right by me? What do you know about me?" Her eyes were narrowed. She had never been angrier than she was now.

When he didn't answer, she pressed on his shoulder.

"Ow! Stop that!" He moved away from her.

"I'm getting your attention, because I *am* going to get an answer."

"We need to get moving."

"You can't do that without me and I want an answer." She settled down beside him, more than ready to wait him out.

Davd looked at her for a long moment. "You want to stay out here longer than you need to?"

"No, I want to be home with my family and friends and I want a bath, but I wasn't given that choice. How do you know anything about me?"

Davd shifted uncomfortably, but sighed. "We, we've been watching you since Puter decided that you should be an enforcer and have no children."

She stared at him, rendered speechless for an instant. There were just too many questions to ask.

She started at the beginning. "We? You're not that much older than me, and why?"

"Kat." She stared at him. He'd never called her by her name before. She hadn't realized he even knew it. "Think about it. Your ancestors were some of the most brilliant people on Rth. They were part of the team that put this colonization project on track and made it happen. They were brave enough to come out here themselves and get everything started. Why the frak would some memory chips and wires decide that those genes should die out? Your grandmem is legendary for the work she's done in the medical field here. Why would someone like her still be on the front line instead of teaching, research? And your Grandda Chi—the two of them should have had a dozen children, but Puter decides they should have two and one of them shouldn't reproduce at all? The other had one child, you, and you're not supposed to have children. You explain that logic to me."

She stared at him for a long moment. How did he know all of this about her? "There, there has to be a reason. Maybe Da and Aunt Castra didn't inherit what was needed. I obviously I didn't have what it takes to be a doctor—"

"Obviously?" He looked down at his arm. "No, that's not obvious to me at all. I'd have bled to death without you. Not only did you kill the liger, you knew exactly what to do with a traumatic wound *and* the guts to do it. Does that sound like someone who doesn't have what it takes to be a doctor? You can't tell me you don't still wonder about it. Why else would you have those supplies in your pack?"

She sat staring at him for a long moment. He had a point. Why had she never...

"Kat?"

"I don't... You're right, we need to get going." She began gathering up the food scraps and cleaning up. Be a doctor? After all this time, surely that dream was long buried. Why was she even thinking like this?

She refused his help in taking down the tent, so he visited with the horses and gave her assistance and guidance in packing and saddling the horses.

He stepped forward to help her up on the horse but she moved without him and seated herself without his aid.

"The trick is going to be getting you up here," she said looking around.

"I can do it."

"Yeah, right." She moved the horse toward a large root that was sticking up out of the ground and motioned for him to climb it. He seemed impressed and followed her directions. With his injured arm in a sling, she helped hoist him into the saddle. He settled himself against her, his good arm around her waist. She stiffened, he felt good behind her, kind of like the way it had felt in his arms this morning. It was a necessity; put it aside.

She rode back to the packhorse and gathered up those reins.

"You're a quick learner," he commented.

"Good thing for you," she retorted and moved out in the direction Davd indicated.

Chapter Twenty-Five

They traveled for a while before she became aware of the change in things. She didn't move, analyzing. Oh Gault! Was that... she squirmed, trying to put some distance between them and he groaned.

"Don't move."

"Is that—"

"I can apologize, or you can be flattered, but please don't move around so much."

"I'm getting down." She pulled up on the reins and practically flew off the horse. When she turned, his eyes were closed. She glanced down and her own eyes widened. When he opened his eyes, it was to her scarlet face, her eyes riveted to his groin.

He cleared his throat and she jerked away.

His dismount was a great deal less graceful than hers, stumbling when he reached his feet. He grabbed hold of the saddle with his good arm and she moved forward quickly to steady him. Her hand went to his forehead. He might be a little warm but no real fever.

"I'm okay."

She only nodded. "Let's stop for lunch."

"It's early."

"Deal with it." She was already walking away from him.

She watched him sigh as he took seat against a nearby tree. Her frantic need to get away from him had apparently taken care of his "problem."

Kat handed him the water container and some antibiotics, then let the horses graze as she prepared lunch. She could feel him watching her silently. He took the food with a nod of thanks, and watched as she took a seat across from him leaving plenty of space.

****

Okay, maybe he wasn't her type, but there was no reason to have *that* reaction to him. While he'd never found anyone he wanted to contract, he'd managed to meet a lot of available women. None had reacted to his attentions like that.

Of course, Puter decreed that she not reproduce. Usually that meant a lot of uncommitted sex, at least in his experience it did. He'd enjoyed that benefit for a long time.

The silence was getting heavy when he looked up. Fratz, he might as well clear the air. Since they were sharing a horse, they had to be in close proximity. "Have you ever had sex?"

"What?" She sputtered, obviously shocked by the question. "Of course I have!" Her indignation was clearly not feigned. The topic didn't seem comfortable to her though, which surprised him. Most of the women he knew talked about it all the time.

"Did you enjoy it?" Everyone he knew enjoyed it and they were going to be together on that horse for at least one more day. The feel of her body against his aroused him. Was he supposed to apologize for that?

"Why the fratz would you care?"

"Because, well, because I do. Did you enjoy it?" he repeated.

"It was okay."

"Okay?"

She just stared at him.

"So you didn't *enjoy* it. Did you have an orgasm?"

"What the—Are you *analyzing* me? I'm your captive, that doesn't give you permission to ask personal questions. This is absolutely none of your business and I don't—"

"Maybe I don't deserve it, but indulge me." Her reaction caught his attention even more. "Did you have an orgasm?"

"I suppose so."

He closed his eyes, shaking his head. "No, you didn't."

"And you know that how?"

"Because you would know."

"You know this because of your vast experience with women, I suppose." Her eyes were narrowed.

"I, uh, have some experience in the area." She looked away first. Her cheeks looked heated. "And you?"

"What?"

"How did you get your experience?" he asked softly.

"That's none of your business."

"Indulge me, please. We're kind of friends now, right? We've saved each other's lives. That should count for something. Are you more attracted to women?"

She opened her mouth apparently to give him some sharp retort, but then just closed it again, and returned to her meal. He'd just about given up when she glanced up at him again.

"The doctor 'deflowered' me. That's what she called it anyway."

"The doctor *raped* you?" He felt fury grow in him, catching him off guard. Why did he want to know any of this?

"No, no, she used some sort of... instrument. It hurt, but she said it was the best way. Then she said I should find someone to... to stretch me before I..."

"Oh Gault. I'm sorry."

"There's nothing to be sorry about. I won't be having children, so it's not a big deal."

"Kat, you are a beautiful, sensuous woman. You should—"

She looked at him, stunned for an instant. What had he said that would cause that expression?

"Don't worry about it."

"I *am* worried about it."

"Look, I know biology. We'll, it'll be okay."

"You thought that was just biology?"

"Are you going to try to make me believe you're attracted to me? Don't bother. I don't have a fragile ego."

"That's not—Why wouldn't I be attracted to you?" he asked her, more than curious at her reaction.

"You're supposed to reproduce. Puter said you should have one son. I can't do that, so there'd be no reason to be attracted to me."

"That not the only reason people make love," he said gently.

"Make love? I thought we were talking about sex."

"Look, I'm sorry. I didn't mean to make you uncomfortable. You're right, I shouldn't have pressed. We should get moving. The sooner we get to the settlement the better. We have at least one more night out here."

****

She nodded and began clean up. How the fratz had they had a conversation like that? They weren't friends, she'd never even confessed that information to Bree. What made her talk to *him* about it? She didn't want anything to do with him, did she?

He seemed better now that he was riding in front, at least at first. He'd grown quiet and distant now, despite or maybe because of the fact they were still pressed up against each other.

"Davd? Are you okay?" she finally got up the nerve to ask.

"Great."

She nearly drew back at his short, clipped response, but he seemed flush. She was still concerned about his wound. "I don't think so. What's wrong?"

"What's wrong? This!" He grabbed her hand from around his waist and pressed it against him. She gasped and jerked her hand away. He felt like warm steel under her hand and larger than before.

He pulled up on the reins and slid off the horse. She kept her seat for the moment, just watching him. He began to pace.

"What did you expect?" he growled at her.

"I thought—"

"What? You thought your arms around me, your breasts pressed into my back, your warm breath on my neck. Yeah, no reason for me to be affected." What was wrong with him, did he always react to women this way? Was it because she was so obviously not interested in him? It didn't feel that way.

"Davd—"

"I want you. Okay? It's not lust, and no, I'm not going to force myself on you. It's not my style."

"I didn't think that."

"Of course you did. Look, we might as well stop for the night. It's a little early, but we shouldn't overtax the horse."

"How much longer?"

"We'll be there around lunch time tomorrow."

She nodded and dismounted. Needing to change the subject, she said, "I can't believe you found a place this far from everything."

He looked up startled and his face grew red. "It, it's not really that far away."

"We've been out here for days."

"I, uh, I took the long way, to get you confused."

She stared up at him.

"I know, sorry. By the time I got hurt, it was too late."

"Real smart."

"Yeah, everything about this has been real smart."

She looked away then. Whoever planned this couldn't have known what they were doing. Why her? Why had they been watching her all these cycles? Fratz! He began unloading the tent and she moved to his side. "Let me."

"I can do it."

"I'm sure you can, but please, let me." She put her hand on his arm and he looked down at it.

"Not afraid of me?" It was a sneer.

She met his eyes. "No, I'm not."

He looked abashed then and shook his head. "Sorry."

"I don't think either of us is used to spending quite this much time with other people."

"Well, not like this anyway," he agreed.

****

They set up the tent and he handled the horses while she got their dinner together. He kept his arm in the sling, but he could feel that it was better already. The scab-like covering that the clotter had become, was already beginning to flake away at the edges.

He mentioned that when they sat down to eat and she smiled. "Let me see."

He obediently exposed his shoulder for her, giving her a wink and slight bump and grind. She huffed and tried to hide her smile. "I'm getting to you, aren't I?"

"It's your sterling personality, no doubt." She took the empty container from him.

It was strange. One of his rules was that no woman stayed overnight at his place and he rarely stayed over with them. It was just sex. But this time with her had been enlightening. Obviously they were both loners, but they had adapted to being together. She could easily have let him bleed to death out here, but instinctively she had protected him. He, in turn, had tried to protect her. He found that in spite of everything, he liked her and enjoyed her company. That was a new one.

"Tell me, if we had gone the 'short' way, how long would we have been out here?"

"Uh, one night."

She stopped, the containers seemingly forgotten in her hands and just stared at him. "One? Are you serious? We've been out here for almost four—"

"I told you, the long way. You needed time to get acclimated."

"Acclimated? Yeah, you keep telling yourself that. Am I," she looked down at the empty container, but continued. "Am I going to be living in a tent for the rest of my life?"

"No, Kat it's not like that. This settlement is cycles old. We have houses with plumbing and everything."

"That'll be a nice change."

"Thought you'd like it."

Her smile faded. "Davd, I have to go back."

That caused a stab in the gut that caught him off guard. What was he thinking? Gault, he would miss her. "I'm, we're hoping you won't want to."

She turned away then and finished the clean up. A gust of wind caught the part of her hair that had come out of her braid. It was cold and she shivered. Davd looked around.

"I think some weather is blowing in."

"What do you mean?"

"Cold weather. We'll need to bundle up tomorrow."

"The planet doesn't want us to get to this damn settlement."

He grinned. "It does look that way. Come on, the temperature is dropping. Let's get in the tent."

"Will the horses be okay?"

He faced her, surprised. "Yeah. I'll strap a blanket on them, but they'll be fine. Go on in."

The temperature *was* dropping. The sound of the wind flapping the tent seemed to make it worse. She might have to get her jacket out again. It was covered in blood, but she was cold.

"Come here." Davd moved toward her. "The horses are huddled together; you don't think they're smarter than us?"

She looked at him, her arms tight around herself.

"Kat, come on. I told you, I want you but I'm not going to force myself on you. I don't do that.

You're my friend now. I guess my first female friend. I don't want to hurt you. Please, trust me."

His friend? Well, yes, he supposed on some level they were friends now. She wasn't that hard to be around and she gave him as much space as she could. He had to admit he admired her, he might have more experience being far from "civilization," but she was catching on quick. He watched her take a deep breath and moved closer, letting his arm go around her with both sets of bedding covering them. It *was* warmer.

Chapter Twenty-Six

After the most restful night yet, cozily warm against one another, they woke to a cold morning. It didn't mean anything, they were just surviving she reminded herself. He shared his extra clothing with her and they moved swiftly to break camp and get moving.

They made good time, and she could see the outer edge of the settlement in a couple of hours.

She pulled his jacket closer around herself and decided the hell with it, holding tight to him for warmth and security as he rode into the settlement. People were coming out of the houses and hurrying to meet them in the courtyard in the center of the buildings.

He had been right, these were real buildings. They weren't metal like she was accustomed to, but they looked sturdy. In fact, they looked like they belonged, a part of the landscape. Most of the buildings were small, though there were two much larger buildings that seemed to grow up out of the ground at the far end of the settlement. The roofs twinkled in the mid-day sun.

"You okay?"

She jumped even though his voice was low, reassuring.

"I guess so."

"They're glad to see you. They want you here, remember that."

"Davd! We were beginning to worry." A tall man, older than Davd, put his hand on the horse's neck and patted it.

"You'd have good reason." He dismounted and reached for Kat's hand. She looked around the group of people that were beginning to assemble. Her grip on his hand tightened. She stood beside him, back straight.

"Kat," the man held out his hand to her. "I'm Gart. I act as mayor of this community. Welcome."

When she didn't respond, Gart looked over at Davd. "Is everything okay?"

Davd stepped closer and lowered his voice. "Not exactly. It was a rough trip. We lost a horse." Gart looked over at the horses that were being led away to confirm that. "We were attacked by a liger. She killed it, and for the record, she didn't shirk."

Gart's eyes widened. "Didn't—"

Davd nodded.

"Inside, now." He turned and walked rapidly toward the large building to the left. Kat looked over at Davd, who nodded. Gart opened the door to his office and motioned for both of them to enter. Another man, slightly younger than Gart, and an older woman entered as well, shutting the door.

"What happened?" Gart demanded as he took a seat behind the desk.

"I got... different instructions after our last meeting. I was ordered to shirk. Kat was given the assignment to bring me back. I was told to bring her here."

Gart's mouth had fallen open. The older woman stepped forward. "You can't go back?"

He shook his head and Kat looked over at him startled. "You can't..." She shut her mouth then and waited.

"Who gave you those orders?" Gart demanded.

"Ralt, uh Head."

Kat nearly gave herself whiplash turning back to him. "Head? My supervisor, Head?"

He looked uncomfortable, but he nodded.

"We need to speak in private. I'm sorry, Kat, but if you will—"

"No."

Gart blinked, obviously unused to being spoken to in that manner. Davd looked down and she glanced over at him. He was hiding a smile! Son of a—

Instead of making an issue of it, Gart looked over at the two strangers in the room. The woman nodded and he took a deep breath. "We'll do this later. Please forgive our inhospitality. Why don't the two of you freshen up? Have Marm take a look at your shoulder."

"Not necessary. Kat took excellent care of me." Davd rose and Kat was right behind him. He touched her elbow to lead her out of the heavily silent office and out to the courtyard.

"What the frak is going on?" she hissed at him.

Before he could respond, she heard a man call to her. "Kat! You're here!"

The man came running up and drew her into a hug. She pulled back when he released her. "Mi-Mikeal? Is that you?"

The man grinned nodding. Kat realized that Davd's body had stiffened and that he seemed to be appraising Mikeal. "You were the first person I thought of when I got here."

"When you—Me? Why?"

"Puter did the same thing to you he, *it* did to me. Everyone knew you wanted to be a doctor like your grandmem, but Puter... I'm sure you were a great enforcer, but I *wasn't* great at agriculture. Now you'll be able to do what you really want to do with your life. You'll be such an asset to this place."

Kat blinked, but she could feel a bemused smile beginning to form on her face.

"Where are you staying?" Mikeal asked.

"With me." Both Kat and Mikeal turned. Davd's face was stone and he had sounded... dangerous. Mikeal actually took a step back, then looked embarrassed.

"Oh, of course. We can catch up later. I'm sure you want to get settled. See you at dinner." He squeezed her hand again, nodded to Davd, then left them at a near run.

"My house is over here." He started walking toward a cluster of houses. They were all similar, one story with small porches on the front. The glitter of the roofs caught her eye again and she realized they were covered with solar collectors.

She hesitated a moment, then followed. After a few steps, Davd settled his shoulders and turned back to make sure she was behind him. Was he angry with her? Maybe she shouldn't have spoken with Gart that way, but it hadn't seem to bother him at the time. "You probably still want that bath. The water should be warm by now."

"How? You haven't—"

"I saw people headed toward the place when they recognized us. I'm sure they got everything set up for us." He stepped up onto the small covered porch and opened the door allowing her to enter. He seemed better now and obviously proud of this structure. She didn't know him that well. She was probably imagining things.

She looked around with interest. There was a main room, which covered the entire front of the house. The walls were logs, bark removed and rubbed smooth on the inside. The furniture was handmade and completely different from anything she had ever seen before. All furniture was identical in the arcologies. These were beautifully made as well as functional. Decorations were carved into the arms and legs of the chairs and settee, and the cushions were bright and colorful. A woven multi-colored cloth hung on one wall as decoration. The room was the full length of the house and probably four and half meters deep. There was a skylight in the roof, so the room was bright with afternoon sun. Two doors led off the room.

"The bath is here." He opened the door on the right. It was a good size room with a sink, tub and toilet. A skylight lit it during the day as well. She saw candles near the tub and beside the sink. Shelves, holding a couple of towels, lined one wall. "The bedroom is the other room."

"How did you get a tub here?" she asked, incredulous.

He grinned. "One of the processes we haven't bothered to use since we landed. It's made from the insulation that we use around the main pipes. It molds nicely and once it hardens, it's water proof and virtually permanent. Just be sure you put the pipes in place first." He opened the valve to let water pour from the boiler into the tub.

"Toss your clothes out there and we'll get them cleaned. In the meantime, I'll find something warmer than your uniform for you to wear. I'll be back before you're out of the tub."

"Where are you going?" she asked quickly.

"I'll bathe next door at Carla's."

"Carla?" Her voice sounded frosty suddenly. That surprised her, why should she care with whom he chose to bathe.

"Yeah, Carla, she lives next door. She's Gart's mem."

"Gart's *mem*?"

"Yeah, she's kind of everyone's mem here. She's great."

She saw the look of affection on his face and relaxed. "I'll see you in a little while then."

He seemed to come back to himself and turned immediately toward the door. "Yeah, see you in a few minutes."

Bemused, she watched him leave, then looked over at the tub and immediately began stripping. She undid her braid and massaged her scalp as she lowered herself into the warm water. Damn, that felt good.

She washed her hair first and was mortified to find leaves stuck in it. What kind of impression could she have made on these people? He could have said something. She scrubbed down, then let the water out and began refilling it. Clean, she just lay in this second water and relaxed, letting her thoughts drift.

When she heard the door to the house open, she reluctantly rose from the water and dried herself off. The only thing to wear in the bathroom was a robe, his of course, but she wrapped it around her, tying the sash with a knot.

"You okay in there?" Davd called.

She couldn't help the smile. His voice had become familiar and welcome in this strange place. She would not be admitting that to him, however. She opened the door and saw his eyes scan her in his robe. "Better, how about you?"

He was wearing ods and a thick shirt, the clotter was completely gone now. His hair was wet and slicked back. She approached him. "Let me see your shoulder."

He pulled the shirt away from his shoulder and, as she checked him out, sniffed her. "You smell better."

She cut her eyes toward him. "The wound looks good. The scars aren't going to be bad. And for the record, you smell better too."

He grinned. "Hungry?"

"I could eat. At least I could eat something besides those pack meals."

"You don't like my cooking?"

She looked up at him. "No."

"Well, go ahead, insult me. See if I care. I brought you some of Carla's clothes. They're in the bedroom. Go ahead."

She entered the room he indicated and looked around. None of the ceilings in the house were very high; taller than him, but short enough to keep the heat down in the living area. There was another skylight here in the bedroom, but no windows the same as the bath, so during the day no additional lighting should be needed. The bed was the largest thing in there, with a colorful covering that matched the cushions in the main room. Shelves lined the wall on both sides. His few pieces of clothing, now folded, took up little space on the shelves on the far side of the room. The shelves on this side of the room were mostly bare, as though waiting for something or someone. His shoes were on the floor under his clothes.

When she emerged, she was wearing ods with a soft, padded shirt over a long sleeve t-shirt. Surprisingly, the pants were long enough. She wanted to meet this woman. If someone old enough to be Gart's mem shirked, Kat could learn a few things from her. She stopped short at that thought. She wasn't an enforcer anymore, was she? She didn't have to think about that, unless of course she returned. That was what she wanted, wasn't it? She couldn't just abandon everything she knew for strangers. Why was she involved in this at all? Why had Head done this to her?

"Kat? What's wrong?"

"Uh, nothing, just thinking. I have a lot of questions."

"Turns out, so do I."

"You really can't go back?"

He shook his head. "I thought Gart knew about this. I thought it was planned, like all of my missions. It makes me think Head's in trouble."

She stiffened immediately. "How do you know Head? Why would he be giving you orders? You have Cal."

"Head's my uncle. My Mem's brother, Ralt. After my da left, he helped raise me. He wasn't allowed to reproduce himself—another huge mistake on Puter's part."

"I can't disagree with you there. We need to find out what's going on. If he needs help..." She stopped, what was she about to say?

He stopped, looking closely at her. "You'd work with me on that?"

"Yes. He's important." Well he was and he'd been her advocate on more than one occasion.

"He feels the same about you. I'd like to hear that story sometime."

"He helped me. I can't repay what he did, but I want to try."

Davd nodded. "Come on, it's dinner time. We all eat at the big building. I don't have a kitchen here."

"I noticed that."

"It's more efficient. And maybe there are better cooks here than me."

"You think?"

His eyes narrowed but she grinned at him. "Come on. Put on my coat, the temperature is really dropping. We got here just in time."

Chapter Twenty-Seven

They lost no time rushing over to the largest building at the end of the square, into what looked like utter chaos. She shrank back slightly at the crowd and noise. So many children. She'd never see so many outside of the school floor.

"It's okay," he said reassuringly. He led her to one of the long tables and seated her on a bench. "I'll get our meal."

This building was constructed, as his house had been, out of logs. But on a much larger scale than his home. There were at least ten large tables and other smaller ones scattered around. Again, the walls were decorated in lovely colorful woven hangings and the posts were carved with all manner of animals and symbols. There was a second floor to this building, so there were no skylights, but lamps gave off generous light. It took her a moment to realize that the lamps were placed in front of reflective material, enhancing the light produced.

Food was brought in and placed on serving tables. The villagers lined up, chatting and visiting, as they took their meals and looked for places to sit.

It seemed as though half the people in the large room came by and spoke to her. She realized that she was totally unaccustomed to socializing on this level. Her normal pattern was to eat with Bree and Danl once a week. Gramma Lil once or twice. She didn't go out with others very often, it was easier and more comfortable to spend an occasional evening with Bree and now their new baby, Drew. Other types of evenings seemed to lead to alco-drinks and offers of sex. That kind of "fun" never attracted her. Davd had come too close to a truth she'd given no thought. Wasn't sure she wanted to now.

How had he known those things about her? She hadn't known them about herself.

There were children everywhere here, as well as young adults, who were playing or flirting with each other. She, however, was enthralled at the number of babies, from little ones barely able to walk all the way down to infants. There were two women obviously pregnant. One looked ready to burst any minute, in her opinion.

She was the one that approached Kat. "Hello, I'm Dana. It's wonderful having you here. You can be a big help to us. Have you ever delivered a baby?" Her hand lovingly caressed her swollen belly. Gault, did everyone here know everything about her?

Davd came up with two plates then and heard the question.

"Uh, no, not alone."

"Well, you'll certainly get some practice around here. Welcome." She smiled and waddled off. Davd laughed when he looked at her.

"Where the fratz have you brought me?" she hissed at him.

"Colonization central. We're growing here, not like back there."

"No fratz." She took her plate from him and he sat beside her. She saw Mikeal come in and nodded when he waved, but didn't motion him over. Davd's reaction to him last time had confused her.

People did give them a little privacy to eat, but that didn't last long. The food was good, different, like the bread and cheese he fed her on the way here. There were spices or seasonings that were fresher or something. In any case, it was different from the food she had eaten her whole life at home, more... real.

Davd looked up and grinned. "Good?"

"What is this? I've never—"

"It's deer meat with vegetables out of—"

"Deer? You mean like the horses but smaller?"

"Well, these are native to the planet, not thawed. There's a herd near here and occasionally they have to be thinned out. It's good lean protein and tastes incredible, which from your expression, I think you agree."

"It, it tastes... wild, free."

He blinked at that. "I suppose it does. It's not processed like everything in the boxes. It was killed with respect, cleaned, and every bit was used for something around the settlement. Now that I'll be living here, I'm going to want to add to my winter wardrobe with the hide of a deer. Since I traveled back and forth, I always kept my uniform and borrowed clothes when I was here for more than a day or two."

She opened her mouth to ask some more questions, but Gart joined them as they were finishing their meal. "I do need to talk to you, Davd."

"You can talk to both of us. We're both trained as enforcers. You might as well use our expertise. Do you think Ralt, uh Head, is in trouble?"

"He has to be. He changed the arrangements and didn't inform us. He's working on his own."

"Have you tried to contact him?"

"We've left messages at the regular places. There's not a lot we can do tonight. It's already starting to snow and I think it's going to be a heavy one. Take a few supplies with you back to your place. Do you have wood?"

"Yeah, someone filled the box for me and I saw several pieces of long wood. We'll be good. If you hear from Ralt—"

"I'll let you know immediately."

Davd rose and Kat followed him. He took the sack of supplies a woman handed him and made sure that Kat was bundled up in his coat. A scarf appeared from someone and she wrapped it around her head. She'd never been outside and weather like this looked rough.

With his arm around her, he hurried her back to his house. Once inside, she left his coat on while he lit a fire in the stove. "I was going to do the gentleman thing and offer to sleep out here, but under the circumstances, I don't think that's a good idea."

Rather than dwell on that, she asked, "What's long wood?"

He looked up and grinned. It felt like he did a lot of that when looking at her. The thing was, she wanted to reciprocate. "It's a native wood. We've started growing some Rth trees here, but there's a native wood that burns for a very long time. A good size tree can last weeks if the house doesn't have little children or the elderly. They use it too, but add other woods to get the temperature up quicker and keep it there. We've found a lot of native materials that we use. Puter doesn't seem to want us to know about them.

"You haven't gotten to look around, but there's a large greenhouse to the west. I've worked there a little. It's where we started most of our crops around here. Now, of course, we have fields."

"I thought we weren't supposed to harm the land, but you must have chopped down hundreds of trees."

"Actually, no. The village is in a natural clearing. Almost nothing was cut down for the area. Having a natural spring helped. They did the same with the fields. We're not large enough to need vast fields yet. If we had some of Puter's help and machines, we might never need them, but," he shrugged, "we can't turn there for help. You asked about long wood, it was discovered almost immediately and the settlers realized how well it worked, so that reduced the amount of wood needed for fuel by over three-quarters from what had been projected. The houses did take wood, but I know for a fact that at least one tree was planted for each one cut, in some cases three or four. There's an orchard not far from here, where some native trees were harvested and replanted with Rth trees. We have apples, pears, cherries and stuff that we planted to replace what we used. You ate some of the fruit tonight. The people that set up this colony knew what we'd caused on Rth. Those things were considered, thought out and planned. We *can* learn. Now it's the norm to appreciate nature and defend it. Everything is used, even the smallest scrap of wood from the trees we did take is important." He shook his head. "They had me making wedges and biscuits out of the leavings on one of my trips. You'd be amazed how much wood is gotten from just the fallen limbs."

She looked up at the skylight. In the deepening twilight, it didn't emit much light.

"Do you worry about that leaking?"

"No. It's made of the same plastic as the windows; it's not going to break. The wood will rot before anything happens to that pane. We just make sure it's well caulked."

Davd lit a large lamp on the only table. A warm glow lit the room.

"Thanks."

He grinned. "It should start warming up in here soon." He took the supplies over to the table and left them, then turned abruptly. "I forgot to have Carla lend you something for sleeping."

"Oh, well, uh, that's okay. I can sleep in these."

"I think my robe will be more comfortable. Go on, get ready. I'll wait out here."

"Well, there is more room than in the tent. Hey, are the horses going to be okay?"

"Yes. Thank you for thinking of them. They're in a barn tonight, much warmer and there are other horses to keep the body heat up."

"Good, well, I'll—" she motioned toward the bedroom and disappeared inside. When she reemerged in his robe, he was watching her.

"You okay?"

She nodded. "How come it's warmer in the bedroom?"

"You haven't had time to look at the construction around here—"

"And I wouldn't understand it if I had," she interrupted.

"Possibly true, but we're using a lot of designs that were developed on Rth to use the environment instead of exploit it. The back of the house faces north, so there are no windows back there, even with the plastik we use. And the outer wall is bermed, that means it was built partially underground to use a natural insulation. And we installed geothermal heat in the floors of all of the first floor rooms. Some houses, where there are more kids, have bedrooms upstairs, but I didn't need anything that big."

"Smart."

"We think so. I'm gonna get ready for bed. Sit here near the stove."

She took the seat he indicated and watched him disappear into the other room. It was getting warmer, so she rose and moved to the window. It was the real outside, not like those panels in the apartments at home. The snow was coming down now and blowing in all different directions.

That's where he found her. "Pretty, isn't it?"

She jumped a little, but nodded. "How did you get windows? Did you say this was plastik?"

"Yes, it's the leftovers, the shards of the plastiks that are made in the arcologies. It weighs almost nothing, so whenever one of us makes a trip inside, we bring it back. We had some with us."

"Makes a trip inside?"

"We can talk about that tomorrow. I'm sure you're tired. Come on." He held out his hand but she hesitated. "Kat?"

"Yeah, I..."

"We shared body heat when we were out on the trail. What's different?"

"Nothing, but..."

"But with a real bed, you don't think you can trust me," he said quietly.

"No, that's not... We really don't know each other."

He looked startled at that. "We've just spent one of the most intense weeks I've ever had, together. Okay, yes, I kidnapped you, but it was because Ralt told me to. I think he was trying to get you out, because something was happening. He wanted to make sure you and I were safe."

She realized she was afraid, but was it fear of him or fear for Head?

"Kat, talk to me."

"Sorry. I'm being stupid. Let's go on to bed, if we remember how to sleep in an actual bed."

He took her hand. "I'm still on my best behavior. Remember, anything else is not my style."

"Right. I bet you take up most of the bed, don't you?" He had in the tent.

"Well sure. I sleep alone."

"Great," she muttered.

He picked up a pair of tongs from beside the wood box and lifted a smooth rock from the top of the stove.

"What are you doing?"

He didn't answer, but she followed him into the bedroom.

"Which side do you want?"

"The right, I don't want to hurt your shoulder."

"The right it is, but my shoulder is good. You're a great doctor." She felt the flush of her face and he seemed to be staring. Would it be okay for him to stay in here all night? He ran the hot stone over the sheets.

"Nice," she said.

"Hey, we're very modern here. Get in before it cools off, I'll be right back." He returned the stone to the stove and hurried back to her. "How is it?"

"Comfortable. It's got the ground beat all to fratz."

He grinned and crawled in beside her. "Do you mind me being here?"

"It's your bed."

"That's not what I asked."

"I know. It feels different. Five days ago I didn't know you, then you kidnapped me and dragged me away from everything I've ever known."

"Kat—"

"I know, you had instructions. Then you nearly get killed saving my life and I—"

"You save me."

She looked up at him and gave a tiny shrug.

"It was a big deal to me," he commented.

"Now I find out the whole thing was orchestrated, possibly to save me from the beginning though we don't know from what, and now we're in bed together."

"Well, I like that last part."

She huffed and rolled over, turning her back to him. He curled himself around her and, after a few minutes, she did relax.

Chapter Twenty-Eight

She woke slowly, in itself unusual, and very well rested. It took a moment to realize that the soft, smooth caress of a hand on her stomach wasn't a dream. Memory returned then and she looked around to find Davd still curled around her, watching her. She tensed.

"Morning," he said with a smile. "Warm enough?"

"Uh, yeah." Why was he touching her like that? And why did it feel so good?

"Excellent. I'm going to see how much snow we got." He leaned in and to her astonishment, kissed the tip of her nose. He then eased himself out of bed, keeping her covered, and padded to the other room. She watched him go with confusion and, okay she had to admit it, mild regret.

What was she thinking?

He popped his head back in the door. "It's still coming down. We must have twenty centimeters. Want some breakfast?"

He sounded so young and happy, as though it were a holiday. Twenty centimeters of *snow*? Wouldn't that paralyze the community?

"I'm going to heat the bread a little. Just wait there."

Uncertain what to do, she did wait. He joined her in a few minutes, with cheese on lightly toasted bread.

"It's a good thing they sent supplies with everyone last night. I'll be able to get out if we need more, but you're not used to it."

"Do we need to check in or something?"

"They'll see the smoke from the chimney. If we're needed, they'll ring the bell."

"Bell?"

"At the dining hall. Don't worry. I don't have regularly assigned chores, because I've not been a full-time resident. Guess that'll change now. You should get dressed, then come in the main room. It's warmest."

"What are we going to do today?"

"I'm going to unpack. This place hasn't had many personal touches, but I took a few minutes to grab some things before I left—"

"The picture of you and your uncle."

He looked surprised for a moment. "Yes. I guess you were at my apartment."

"Standard procedure. I met M'gan. You stood her up."

Davd chuckled. "I guess I did. Wonder what that will do to her ego?" He seemed to dismiss her quickly from his mind. "Anyway, I have some of my favorite printed books, a few things that I managed to pack. I need to make sure they're okay."

She nodded and he left her again. He certainly hadn't seemed to give M'gan much thought. For some reason that made her feel warm. She swallowed the last bite of her breakfast and rose from the bed. It was chillier than she was used to, but not uncomfortably so.

She dressed quickly, pulling on a pair of drawstring pants borrowed from Carla, and taking one of his sweaters from the shelf to tug over her shirt.

She pulled the padded blanket, her Gramma Lil called these things quills, up over the padded mat they had slept on, then she joined him in the main room.

"Hi. Good idea," he indicated the sweater she had chosen. "The bathroom's yours. Should be warm enough."

"Thanks," she said faintly and left him. The bath was less than a third the size of the bedroom, but more than adequate. She took a cloth down from the shelf to wash her face. There was a pitcher to carry warm water from the tub to the sink. There was no need for two boilers in such a small room. She filled the sink and looked around for her pack. A knock on the door surprised her.

"You might want this."

"Uh, thanks." She accepted the pack and shut the door again. She gave herself a mini-bath and re-braided her hair.

Ready to face him now, she emerged to find him standing at the table in the main room. "Did you find your things?" she asked as she joined him.

"Yeah, looks like everything made it without damage. Here's that picture." He handed her a photograph actually printed out on paper. It was him, younger, probably on the day he had graduated as an enforcer. Head, looking just like he did now, had his arm around Davd's shoulders, smiling.

"I've only seen Head smile like that once." Abruptly she recognized him. He was the young man Head had been talking to at that graduation she had attended. Had Head planned to introduce them then? He chose her to "bring him back." There was so much she needed to learn.

"He was really happy that day. I'd made it and I think, no, I know he felt a sense of relief."

"Was your mem there?"

Davd's smile faded. "No. She was already gone."

"How did she die?"

"Liver problems. She was very fond of alco-drinks, especially after Da transferred to Secondport. Puter gave her a new liver the first time, but when she messed up again... " He shrugged and turned back to the table. She kept quiet, not sure what to say. Something tugged at her memory, but she pushed it aside.

"Ralt, sorry, *Head* gave me these books. There aren't that many printed out like this anymore, so they're especially important to me."

"What are they?"

"Old stories, from Rth. I've read them lots of times. This one is called *Treasure Island*. It's about a boy who goes off on a ship with pirates. This is *Les Miserable* about a prisoner—but you don't care about that."

"Actually, I do. I don't know those stories, but Gramma Lil used to tell me stories her parents had told her. Let's see, there was one about an abused girl who meets a prince, Cin-drella or something like that. And one about a woman who sleeps until a prince kisses her. It's been a long time."

"You should write down what you remember. The old stories are getting lost. Out here, we can't take the chance of linking up very often. We don't want Puter to find us."

She nodded, missing her gimp again with all its ready data.

His hand brushed her arm, bringing her back to the present. "Anything you want to do? We can't go outside yet, but—"

Gault! Had she really glanced toward the bedroom? He seemed to be fighting a smile.

"Whatever you want." She couldn't meet his eyes now.

"What I want is to get to know you better. I want you to tell me about your parents and friends. I want to know what you enjoy doing in your spare time and all that kind of thing."

"Why?"

"Well, we're kind of living together, at least temporarily, and—"

"But we're not... not... do people 'date' out here?"

He shrugged. "I guess so, I haven't lived here either. Most people come in as couples if they can. The people that live here came to grow the colony, so they wanted their mates with them to reproduce. People aren't just in contracts here. They really are committed to each other. It's not about casual sex or anything like that."

She squared her shoulders, he'd brought up sex again and he'd made the statement how many times now that forcing her wasn't his style. "Do you want to have sex with me?" she demanded before her courage could desert her.

"No," he said. She knew he was watching her. She tried desperately to keep her face bland, not show the flicker of hurt. She was pretty sure she didn't succeed. "Sex is for amusement after alco-drinks or casual acquaintances that aren't really important. To be honest, I'd like to make love to you."

She looked up and met his eyes then, stunned.

"You're not casual to me, Kat. I know technically we haven't known each other very long, but we've experienced things together that I've never gone through with anyone else. I hope we're at least friends by now. I, I'm beginning to suspect that was part of why Ralt sent you after me."

She nodded, that thought had occurred to her as well. It wouldn't really mean anything, even if they did "make love." Looking as he did, he'd have no trouble finding some unattached woman here, but it was cold and they had nothing else to do. At least that's what she tried to tell herself.

He did smile then, as though reading her mind. "Please, come with me." He took her hand and she followed him back to the bedroom. With the snow covering the skylight, the room was dim, which suited her fine. He left the door open for maximum warmth from the stove and walked her to the bed they had shared the night before.

He lifted his sweater over her head and she shivered. "Cold?"

"No." He kissed the tip of her nose again and began unbuttoning her shirt. "My, my breasts are too small."

He stopped and looked into her eyes. "Who told you that?"

"The last... a guy."

"He was an idiot. Your breasts are perfect," he cupped one through the undershirt she still wore. "They're high and firm and most important, they're real, they're you." He pulled the thin shirt from her and leaned over. He kissed her left breast lightly as his hand caressed the right. "See, perfect."

She was watching him; her face and neck felt hot. He untied the cord that held her pants and let them fall to the floor. He took her hand and she stepped out of them. He kicked them aside and pulled down the quill. She sat on the side of the bed and he reclined beside her.

"Are, aren't you going to undress?" she asked nervously.

"Not yet. This is for you."

She swallowed convulsively. How had this happened? She'd made herself completely vulnerable to him. She, she *trusted* him, whether or not he'd earned it. When had that happened? As an enforcer, she could fight this, but she didn't want to. Slowly she reclined beside him, but she had to admit to herself, she was scared.

His hand trailed down her side as he propped himself on his elbow, looking down at her. She shivered again at the look in his eyes.

"What do I do?" Her question was barely a whisper.

"Nothing. Let me do everything." He knew instinctively that no one had ever talked like this to her, looked at her the way he was. He could see no experience prepared her for this. Her expression reminded him of one of those deer he'd seen on his last hunt. A tenderness for her rose in him. She was giving him a gift, even after the chaos he had caused in her life.

His hand began caressing her softly, sometimes gently kneading her flesh. He wanted to memorize her body. He found her calming under his attentive care.

After she had relaxed, he spread her legs and his hand caressed the curls at her apex. Nervous again, he felt her start to pull away.

"Shh. I'm not going to hurt you."

One of his long slender fingers gently rubbed her folds. She seemed startled to realize she was wet down there. He smiled and allowed his finger slowly to penetrate her most private place.

He didn't want to hurt or scare her. His finger was smaller and the moisture lubricated her. He let a second finger enter her. Finding that bundle of nerves, he stroked it softly, then with more pressure. He saw the wave of sensation crash over her. Her body was out of control, shuddering violently. He watched her hands come up to grab his shoulders, seeking stability. The moment should never end.

He realized his breathing was rapid and shallow, fighting his own release.

Slowly her body relaxed, merely quivering now. She met his eyes. "What did—"

"That was an orgasm. And, I'd say it was your first."

She nodded finally, unable to look away.

"If I ever make my way to Centerport, there are several people I'd like to disembowel," he said conversationally, trying to get his breath back too.

"What?" She blinked, clearly startled at his words.

"Or maybe not. It means I got to share this with you. Those imbeciles didn't deserve you anyway."

A confused smile grew on her face. He found himself actually angry at her former sex partners. How could they have hurt her this way, she didn't deserve that kind of treatment.

"We, we're not finished, are we?" She asked, her hand now playing with the buttons of his shirt.

"Do you want more?"

"Yes." He had to chuckle at the vehemence in her voice and heard the truth.

"You're sure?"

The sound she emitted could only be called a growl, and she had his shirt open. "Careful now, you could hurt me."

She glanced at his shoulder. It was healing nicely.

"I don't mean that." He sat up to remove the shirt and jumped as her hand came to rest low on his abdomen.

"Like this?"

"You're a quick learner."

She didn't answer, tugging at the ods she had already unzipped. He hadn't bothered with underwear and he sprang free as she won her fight with his pants. She stopped then, staring at the size of him.

"Kat, I won't hurt you."

It still seemed to take a while for her eyes to move away from that part of him. He was going to take it as a compliment.

"We can take it slow, or wait until another time."

"No. I don't, I want this now."

His hand caressed her cheek. She trusted him; he could feel it. He leaned in and kissed her mouth again, softly, then let his tongue touch her lips. She opened herself to him and his tongue entered her mouth, finding and dancing with her own tongue. His hands were busy as well. He felt her tightened a little when his finger entered her again. He realized it wasn't from fear this time. Yes, she was still ready. He moved to loom over her and she looked down. He saw her eyes widen. Okay, that ego boost made up for the first time, when she'd literally leapt off a horse to get away from him. He'd promised not to hurt her, but now to make certain of it. Slowly he entered her, not rushing, not shoving his way, but giving her time to adjust to him.

Damn she was tight and he fought for control. Watching her come in his arms earlier had nearly undone him, now he was hanging on by his fingernails. Deeper he explored her and he saw her eyes widen, with pleasure rather than pain. Finally he was there, sheathed completely in her body. He paused, giving her a moment, than he began to slowly retreat.

Her arms tightened around him. "Don't leave—"

"Shh, just relax. Let me pleasure you."

He could see the confusion on her face. No one before had pleasured *her*. He had the distinct impression if she was any more "pleasured" right now she might spontaneously combust. He was moving now, watching her watch him, apparently mesmerized as he slid in and out of her, each thrust deeper than the one before.

His arms were beginning to tremble. He couldn't hold out much longer so one of his hands came to join where they met. He touched that place inside of her again and watched her head fall back and her whole body convulsed. He wondered if she could feel that he too was shuddering as he filled her body with his warmth. He heard himself cry out her name. He never remembered doing anything like that before, had he remembered any other woman's name during sex? He came to rest gently on top of her and held her close as she returned to her body, keeping her safe.

He was slipping under; he thought she was already asleep. He tucked her in next to him, kissed her one more time and managed to snag the quill before he succumbed to sleep.

****

She woke to find herself interwoven with him. One of her legs rested between his legs and she could feel the thickness of him pressed between her leg and his. His arm held her to him and her head rested on his chest. The sound of his heartbeat was steady and soothing.

He had made love to her. Was this what Bree had been talking about? She hadn't really understood what he'd been trying to say to her. She'd had sex, a few times anyway, and hadn't enjoyed it. She hadn't been able to figure out why it was such a popular activity, though she had never admitted that, even to Bree.

The looks that Bree and Danl exchanged made a lot more sense now. Not that she was in love with Davd. No, not at all. There was no need even to think about that, he could reproduce, he was extremely attractive and well liked here in the settlement. And he had kidnapped her—but maybe for a good reason.

Anyway, it was very nice that he'd taken the time with her, to show her what was possible, and oh, what he had done to her body.

"Hi."

She jumped at the sound of his voice. "Uh, hi."

"You okay?"

She smiled then and nodded. His smile was gentle. "I'm glad. You know you're a great lover."

She blinked, "I—"

"You. Your body always knew what it wanted. It just needed to be set free."

Would she ever stop blushing, then she felt his body responding to her again. Her eyes widened as she realized that.

His hand caressed her stomach. "Think I could persuade..."

The rest was cut off by her lips.

Chapter Twenty-Nine

"There's been no contact with Ralt," Gart admitted to Davd after everyone was seated in his office that afternoon. No need to tell Gart about the snowball fight they'd enjoyed on the way over. Now was time for business. "We have to assume he's in trouble. He's never done anything remotely like this before. He must have become aware of something happening and got you out before whatever it was occurred. You're like a son to him and he wanted you safe, you and Kat."

"We have to go back," Kat said it first, but Davd nodded. "We have to get him out and bring him here."

"The trip from Centerport is too—"

"So we get him to Thirdport. I have to go back," Kat repeated. "I have an excuse to have been out of contact. I can go back to Centerport and ask for him to back me up on my assignment."

Davd looked at her, bemused. "You know, that could work."

"Wait," Gart said quickly. "You're talking about pulling *Head* out of Puter's sight? There's no way that won't be noticed."

"So we... we find a way for Puter not to look for him," Kat replied.

Gart looked between the two of them. "Can you pull that off?"

"Yeah, I think we can with Ralt's help. I can't go too far, but Kat's right, she has an excuse for being out of contact. We'll have to head back to Thirdport, the *short* way," he winked at Kat. "Kat can return to Centerport. There's no reason to even contact Cal. You report to Head and he gave you this assignment. You'll have to be careful. Puter hears everything, probably sees everything as well, so if you slip him a note..."

Kat nodded, thinking quickly. "Can I bring anyone else?"

"What?" Gart looked up at her quickly.

"Other people, people to live here?"

"Who?" Davd asked before Gart could. He sounded distant for moment, cool.

"Gramma Lil, for one. If you want a doctor, you can't do any better, and she could teach others what she knows." Kat went silent for moment. She hadn't consciously thought anything like that in a long time. "And Bree and her family. Bree wants children. She and Danl have a son, but Bree should have a dozen. She's a wonderful mother."

Gart just stared at her, but Davd was smiling now. "So, you're not planning on going back."

She jerked, meeting his eyes. She hadn't realized she'd made that decision, but here she was spouting off these plans. "I... I—"

"Good," Davd said softly.

She looked away hoping that Gart hadn't seen her blush. She was moving too fast. This wasn't like her. Was this just because she'd finally experienced good sex? No, that might be part of it, but there was something more—the possibility of being a doctor? There was a freedom she'd never allowed herself to realize was missing from her life and she was just beginning to taste it.

"Gart, let us finalize our plans." Davd broke into her thoughts. "Kat and I are trained for this. We'll report back to you, but let us work it through."

"A large group of people, and *Ralt*, could put us in jeopardy."

"I know that, Gart. Please, let us brainstorm about this."

"I'll want to know your plan. We can't afford to be out of the loop like we were with Ralt's plan."

"I promise."

Reluctantly Gart nodded.

"We have to do this quick, before Kat's absence is too long. I won't put her in danger because of this."

Kat looked over at him and he shrugged. He cared about her. No way was he in love with her, but he did care. She managed to keep her face bland, but inside something seemed to loosen.

"Go on then, make your plans. Report back here after dinner. I believe you're right about hurrying. I'll have you packed for first light."

Kat kept quiet about that. Could they travel in snow like this?

Davd rose and Kat followed him. They were quiet until they got outside. She followed him, using his footprints to trek back to his home. Her best boots were still back in her apartment— another good reason to go back. There were some personal items she wanted to bring with her as well, if she really was going to be living here.

"Davd?"

"Let's get inside."

She nodded and picked up her speed, it was cold and she didn't have the clothing for this. Temperature wasn't a thing she ever thought about, it was unnecessary in the arcology. She'd have to borrow from Carla or someone if they were going to travel in this.

They both stomped the snow from their boots on the porch and headed inside. She moved quickly toward the stove, leaving her coat on. He added more wood; some of the faster burning variety, then removed his own coat.

"Thank you."

He smiled at her. "You're welcome. For what?"

"For being concerned about me. For not wanting Puter to—"

"I'm being selfish. I'm enjoying the company here, a lot."

She looked down at his regard, but smiled.

"You're serious about bringing the others?"

After a moment, she nodded. "They're important to me. Family. And if I can give Bree what she wants most... " She shrugged.

"Okay. Talk to me, tell me what you're thinking."

"I need to go to Head first, I can tell him I've found your nest. He'll know I'm lying then and be watching what I do. I'll have to signal somehow that we're there to help him get away. I'll have to improvise there, but knowing Head, he'll figure it out.

"It's Gramma Lil that worries me. I have to bring her. She would be such an asset."

"I agree. She'll listen to you, won't she?"

"Yes, I think so, but to *shirk*... As for Danl, I don't know where he stands, but I have to give Bree this opportunity. I know he loves her, I think he'll at least give me a hearing."

"Since I don't know any of those people, I can't really give you advice, but from your expression when you talk about them, I think you'll be able to persuade them. Or do what I did," he grinned. He sobered immediately. "There will be a massive manhunt when Head is discovered missing. No one will ever believe that he would shirk, probably not you either, so there might be a rescue mission. That could be dangerous for the community. The people that live here will not go quietly back into a box."

"I agree and there's only one thing I've been able to think of to forestall that."

"Okay, what?"

"You'll have to kill Ralt and me."

Chapter Thirty

The next morning they woke early; early enough to enjoy each other's company once again. The man had taught her so much already. This morning had been no different. She was less shy about her body each time, but this morning truly stunned her.

He had woken her by kissing her stomach and then moved down to kiss her inner thighs and to her astonishment, nuzzled his nose into her curls. But that had been only the first shock. His tongue!

She'd tried to demur. She'd heard of this kind of lovemaking, but no one had ever done it with her, though she had been called upon to do this herself once. To her, it had been easier and quicker than actual sex.

When his tongue had slipped into her, she had jerked, trying to pull away. "You don't have to—"

"Shh, I'm concentrating." He grinned up at her and was back at his task before she could think of anything else to say. He already had her trembling with sensation. "You taste so good."

Her eyes widened, what had he said? He wanted to taste her? He really did seem to be enjoying himself, fratz, she was nearly out of her mind. Then his tongue found that spot he had discovered yesterday. He began flicking at it and she writhed in pure pleasure. Then he pressed on it and the world dissolved. His voice, his caress guided her back.

"I take it that was a first too," he murmured, nuzzling her ear.

She nodded unable to speak, just taking in the contentment of being held safe in his strong arms.

****

The horses didn't seem to mind the snow at all, and in any case, the accumulation wasn't nearly as deep here under the cover of the trees. They moved as quickly as possible. They were going the "short" way this time, but in any case could only afford to spend one night on the road. They wanted to be entering Thirdport first thing the next morning.

There was no reticence about sharing body heat on this trip and he kept her very warm indeed, despite the cold temperature outside of the tent.

They were up before dawn and moving at first light. The arcology came into sight when they had been traveling only a short while. The scope of it from outside caused her to pause. "I knew it was..."

"Big?" he offered.

She cut her eyes toward him. "Yeah, big. Good galt, it's enormous." She had truly had no concept of the size. It hadn't occurred to her that it was round either, since the rooms weren't curved in any way. It was just a huge black cylinder with no visible markings on the outside. The conduits and pipes must be in the curved areas, leaving living space in the more traditional right angles. With no windows, it was difficult to decide in her head where things might be located inside, but rapidly the interior came to her.

"Yeah, it is and a lot of people live in it. This one is the smallest of the three, remember? But look at the size of the planet."

"Hey, you don't have to convince me anymore."

"Good." He leaned over and gave her a kiss. "When we get back, there's a conversation we need to have."

"Conversation?"

"Yeah."

"About?"

"When we get back. Right now we need to head slightly north."

She stared at him for a moment, but it was obvious he wasn't going to continue. He moved on toward the arcology and she urged her horse on as well. "N12, right? Davd, what will the failsafe do to Gram and the baby?"

"Oh, uh, no N8."

"Why N8?"

"It's the one with the failsafe that doesn't work."

She pulled up quickly. "Doesn't work?"

"Right, it's the one we use to go in and out."

"I used N12," she said quietly.

"Yeah, about that. Look, you're an enforcer. I needed the head start. Ralt wouldn't have sent you after me if you weren't good."

"You owe me."

"I promise to pay," he grinned.

"Fraking straight you will." She tried to glower at him, but the realization that he had been concerned about being able to take her was a little bit of an ego soother. "Okay, so I don't have to worry about my friends getting outside, but you're sure transportation will be ready for them."

"Don't underestimate Gart. He's been managing a real colony for a long time. Come on, we don't have any time to waste."

She nodded and they moved on.

It wasn't long before he pulled up again. "This is where we'll leave the horses. We can tie them on a long rein. That way they can eat and get water. Hopefully they won't be alone for long." He moved his horse closer to hers, watching her.

His expression caught her. "I'll be back tonight," she reassured him without thought.

"I'll come after you if you aren't," he said softly.

She looked at him, startled. "You would, wouldn't you?"

"You doubt it?"

She shook her head. "I'll come back, with or without the others."

He closed his eyes at that and leaned over to place his forehead against hers. "Promise?"

"Promise."

He hesitated for a moment, watching her lips, then he pulled back. This woman had certainly gone from annoyance to obligation to important in a short time. Did Ralt really know him that well?

He dismounted and began getting the area ready for the horses. She watched for a moment, then dismounted herself and assisted him.

She had brought nothing with her but her enforcer's pack and even that was lighter than usual. All of her personal belongings, even her personal pack, were back at his house. She would need to move fast and light. She only carried her weapon.

Once the horses were secured, they stood looking at the huge structure in front of them. "Classes haven't started this early, so there shouldn't be anyone on the roof. At least that's the way they do it at Centerport. The gardening is done after sundown."

Davd nodded. "It's the same here."

"Do we run, or move slowly."

"Slowly attracts less attention if there is anyone, but it's more nerve racking." He grinned at her.

"Great. You ready?"

"Yeah." She checked her weapon again and took a deep breath. He took hold of her hand and she turned to smile at him. He took one more kiss. They stepped into the open area together.

They took their time, though it *was* nerve-racking to her to cross the open space. She felt a great deal better when he motioned that they could no longer been seen from the roof, if anyone were there and actually looking. She took a deep breath and they picked up their steps.

He led her to N-8 and she stood behind him as he tested the door. It was still unrepaired and she breathed a sigh of relief. Maybe the jolt wouldn't do

Danl much damage, but Gram was an old woman now and the baby... Once inside, with the door shut, they set down the small packs they were carrying. He opened his, pulled out a small bundle and unwrapped it.

There lay her gimp.

"You're going to need this to get on the shuttle."

She nodded. "Will Puter—"

"You've not been gone that long, especially since you were on a sanctioned search. Obviously you've been in the bowels of Thirdport where there are no stations. As an enforcer, you have that flexibility. Just go on up, get food first, that would be expected since you've been out of touch, living off your pack. Take the first shuttle. You have a lot to get done."

She nodded, more nervous about leaving him than what she was facing suddenly. She turned from him, it had to be done, but he took her arm and turned her back to him. He pulled her against him and kissed her, kissed her like she had never been kissed before.

"Come back to me, Kat, no matter what else."

She nodded, unable to speak for a moment. "I will," she finally whispered.

"Go, now, before I start undressing you again."

She smiled then. "I will be back. I—"

He nodded. "Hurry."

She turned then and moved up the metal stairs. She didn't look back. It would have slowed her too much.
****

He watched until she was out of sight in the dark. It was all he could do not to follow her. Surely she realized the danger she was in, more so than him. Yes, she was well trained, Ralt's mentee. She probably had never realized the things Ralt was teaching her on the side, but they would come in handy now.

When she was out of sight, he picked up his pack and jogged to the right. He had things to complete as well and maybe that would keep his mind off missing her.

They had agreed on a location, W-9, but first the incinerator area would have to be staged. He checked his weapon to ensure it was fully charged. He used quite of bit of the charge on melting the handrail. It needed to look like a major battle had taken place. Then he made a small cut to his left hand and allowed several drops to fall down the front of the incinerator and trail back a few feet toward the stairs. It was a start.

He hurried on toward W-9 after he was satisfied. Puter was careful down here. Even though maintenance was mechanical, trash was non-existent. He needed to find some foam and food wrappers for his nest. He should pass a bin when he headed away from the incinerator and get what he needed.
****

Even *her* legs were tight when she reached the top. She returned to the same exit she had used when she started this adventure and sprinted as she saw the recycler door beginning to close. She barely made it, stopping just outside the door to get her breath. To her immense relief, no one was around this early. She decided to keep moving rather than give away her location this quickly with a food purchase.

She sniffed at the air, what was wrong with it? The answer came to her suddenly. The air smelled stale, not at all like what she had grown accustomed to outside. In her whole life, she'd never noticed that before. It was as recycled as everything else.

Shoving that aside, she moved toward the shuttle station. She was back in her cleaned and pressed uniform. She should look like anyone on the way to work. At the entrance, she finally did use her gimp for a hand-breakfast to eat on the shuttle. It was crowded, but her uniform got her on the first flight. She had a lot to do.

Chapter Thirty-One

Her first stop upon landing was Head's office. She knew he always arrived early, well before his admin, and she definitely needed to see him alone.

She tapped on the door and heard his quick, "Enter." She did and, since she was looking for it, saw the shock in his eyes, quickly hidden. He sat up straight in his chair and fixed his steely eyes on her. "Did you find him?"

"I believe so, sir. I found what I believe to be his nest in the bottom of Thirdport, near W-9." He knew she was lying now, she could see it in his eyes. Would he follow along? "You were right, he's very smart and I'm going to need help bringing him in. I don't believe anyone at Thirdport is capable of the assistance I'm going to need. I realize I'm being presumptuous, but I would like to ask for your assistance. He's very good and if we're going to do this safely... " She let her voice trail off, there was little more she could say without betraying too much.

Head looked at her for a long moment, obviously reading her. She forced herself to keep her expression bland. They both knew they were under surveillance.

"You think you'll need help with this?"

"Sir, sometimes everyone can use a little help."

The man barely blinked. "I'll need some time to get ready, clear my calendar."

"Yes, I've been away for awhile myself. I need to go by my apartment and restock my pack, see my family."

"Of course. Why don't we meet at the shuttle after your evening meal? If this enforcer is in a nest, we'll have a better chance to get him after he's settled for the evening."

"That was my thought, sir. Thank you. I'll see you there."

She nodded and he gave her a small salute, then turned back to his desk.

He'd understood, even quicker than she could have hoped. No wonder he was Head. His decisiveness saved her countless minutes. Now to get to Gramma Lil. Thank goodness this hadn't taken as long as she'd expected.

She hurried to Gramma Lil's apartment. There was a chance she would not have left for work yet, since Head caught on so quickly. She tapped on the door and Lil opened it, already dressed for work.

"I caught you," Kat breathed, hugging her tightly.

"Kat! I was beginning to worry. I haven't seen you in days."

"I know, I'm sorry. Head sent me to Thirdport on a case. It was sudden and it took a little longer than I thought. I have to go back this evening to finish it up, but I wanted to check in and I had an idea. Look, I know you have tons of time off built up. Why don't you come with me? You can visit with Castra and I can join you as soon as this business is over." At least that was what her voice said. She was shaking her head at Lil to keep quiet while she looked around the room.

"Kat?"

"We haven't spent any downtime together lately and this would be perfect. I'm definitely going to be asking for some time off after this assignment." She put her finger to her lips and concerned, Lil followed her lead.

"You know, that's a wonderful idea. I haven't seen Castra in person in ages."

Kat wanted to shut her eyes in relief, but instead smiled broadly. She didn't hang around with idiots. "Great. Look, I have to go to my place and clean up. I just got in this morning and I'll be going back on the evening shuttle. Go ahead and get a reservation for the two of us now. I'll meet you here to help you with your luggage."

"My—"

"Let's plan on several days. Take your large pack." Her eyes went to the large medical pack that Lil carried on emergency calls, staring at it meaningfully. "Make sure it's full with anything you might need. I know there's a play at the main theater in Thirdport that's supposed to be very good, so take your best stuff. Remember that gray sweater thing? That would be perfect."

Again Lil looked confused. Her gray sweater was the heaviest thing she owned. Sometimes she got cold when she had to take an emergency call in one of the uninhabited areas. Kat continued, "Those green heels would be good too."

The only green shoes she own were sturdy boots that she wore to work in construction areas.

"Okay, I can get that stuff together. I need to go into the hospital, to check on some patients after I get the reservation." She picked up her large emergency pack and saw Kat's look of relief.

"Thanks, I'll go get cleaned up and pack a few things too." She hugged her grandmem and whispered, "Take things you want to keep forever, Grandda's pictures. Thank you for trusting me. I promise it'll be okay."

Rather than respond, Lil hugged her tightly. "I'll get that reservation and meet you at the shuttle this evening. Go on, we both have things to do to get ready for our little vacation."

After one last hand squeeze, Kat turned and left the apartment, now headed for her own place. Bree and Danl usually met for lunch on the roof, so that Bree could feed Drew and they could spend some time with him. Hopefully, today would be no exception.

Kat let herself into her apartment and looked around with a new appreciation. She was already stripping off her uniform as she headed for the bath. She didn't know what they had used to get the blood off the jacket, but just in case she would take it back with her. She knew this place would be ransacked once they realized what had happened.

She took a long relaxing shower, enjoying the luxury more than ever, knowing it would be the last one here. Once dressed, she returned to her main room and headed for the shelves. She took down the four printed books she owned. One had been Da's, a copy of several plays from an Rth writer named Shakespierre or something like that—the language was hard to follow but he had enjoyed it. The others were hers, one a present from Gramma Lil that she had been given to her by her own mother, *Grey's Anatomy*, and her older ones, *Grimm's Fairy Tales* and *Pride and Prejudice*. These books had served to hide that disc she had stolen from Gramma Lil so many cycles ago. Then she gathered her printed photos. She had one of her with Grandda Chi and Gramma Lil when she was just a little girl. It had been printed out, as well as one of her and Bree all dressed and excited about going to their graduation. There were no pictures following the graduation.

There was a very good picture of her with Da on the rooftop at the trees and one of her at her second graduation, shaking hands with Head. The last was at Bree's ceremony with the two of them smiling and beautiful. She wrapped them carefully in plastik, then slid them inside of one of her books. She wrapped the books in plastik then and put them on her bed.

Next she pulled out all of her long sleeve tops, ignoring anything dressy that she owned, though she did take a moment to touch the lovely silver dress she had worn at Bree's ceremony. She didn't have any really cold weather clothing, but she could do layers. She slipped them all in a packing bag with the uniform jacket they had cleaned on the bottom and, using the vacuum tube, drew all of the air out of the bag. She did the same with her slacks. She settled them in the bottom of her travel bag with the books packed between them. Her second best boots and two pairs of exercise shoes went on top of that. Her toiletries were on top. There was still a little room, so she put some warm weather clothes on top of that and finally, pressed the closures tight. It would be heavy, but these were the things she really wanted to have with her.

She looked around the apartment. She might have a few more things she wanted to take, and she needed to refill the pack that she carried, but she needed to get to the roof now and find Bree and Danl.

Chapter Thirty-Two

Kat looked official and felt surprisingly calm, when she reached the roof. She spotted Danl and followed him. He waved to Bree and picked up his pace, not seeing Kat. She kept her walk leisurely. There was no reason to draw any attention to herself.

Danl took a seat beside his family as she approached them. Bree looked up and smiled when she saw her. "Hi! Where have you been?"

"I had an assignment at Thirdport. I just got in this morning."

"This morning? You must be exhausted."

"Not too bad. I missed seeing Drew this week, so I couldn't wait. Listen, why don't we move over there. Come on." She plucked Drew from Bree's arms and headed toward a more crowded area. Bree blinked. Kat knew she wasn't acting like herself, but Bree immediately rose, and Danl followed them, with a puzzled look on his face.

Kat took a seat on a bench near the playground. This area was full of children from class on their own lunch break. There was more noise in this area. Bree moved closer to Kat to talk to her. "Kat? Is something wrong?"

Kat dropped her voice and Bree moved in even closer. Danl looked around, picking up on Kat's mood, then took a seat on her other side.

"I don't have time to be delicate about this. I'm sorry, but... have you ever thought about shirking?"

Bree jerked back. "Are you kidding? That's not funny."

"No, I'm not." Kat looked over at Danl. He had gone rigid, his face hard and cold.

"Is this some sort of trap?" he hissed at her. "I never thought you'd—"

"No, Danl, this is no trap." She was watching him closely now and her eyes widened. "You *have* thought about it. Danl, you want to shirk."

His eyes narrowed. "I didn't say that."

"I'm shirking, tonight, I'm going outside," she said quietly, looking him directly in the eye.

"What?" That was Bree. "Don't even joke about—"

"I'm not. That's where I've been. Listen to me; I've been to a village—outside. There are a lot of people there, a lot of *children.* Bree, those women can have as many children as they want. I saw some that had four and more were on the way."

"What are you—"

"Bree, I'm going and Gramma Lil is going with me. She's going to be their doctor and she's going to, she's going to train me to be a doctor too." There, she'd said it aloud. It was real now.

"But Puter said—"

"It's Puter I'm shirking."

Bree's eyes widened, but it was Danl that spoke. "Why?"

Kat faced him, meeting his eye again. "I don't understand it all myself yet, but I am intelligent enough to decide some things for *myself*. I believe I can be a good doctor, maybe not as good as Gramma Lil, but good. I don't think my genes are so bad that they should be lost from the planet just because Puter says so. At least Gramma Lil's genes should continue and I'm the only one that can do that now." She blinked. She hadn't realized she was going to say that either, but it was true. If Davd didn't want to father children with her, there would be someone and Grandda Chi and Gramma Lil would continue here.

Danl watched her for a long moment, seeming to look into her brain, then slowly nodded. "What's the plan?"

Bree turned frightened eyes to him. "Danl? What are you—"

"I know we never discussed this, but we need to go and I believe, no I *know* we'll be safer if we travel with an enforcer."

"You've never—"

"Never talked about this? I'm in a contract with a woman whose best friend is an enforcer. I'm sorry, Bree, I just never thought it would be safe."

Bree just stared at him, open-mouthed.

Danl turned to Kat. "What do we do?"

"Go back to your apartment and pack a few things, nothing fancy. You'll need your sturdiest clothing. You can't pack everything, because you'll be traveling. You'll need warm clothes or layers. Wear several layers and your sturdiest boots. Pack your second best boots and your exercise shoes.

Make it look like you're taking equipment for Drew, but pack extra diapers and clothes instead. Get a reservation for Thirdport for this afternoon. I'll be on the evening shuttle; you need to be there before me. You have relatives over there, don't you Danl? If anyone asks, say you're taking Drew to meet them. Put your luggage in short-term storage when you get to Thirdport then go to the gardens to wait. When it's time for the evening shuttle to arrive, go down and retrieve your luggage. Then meet me at the food kiosk on the north side nearest the recycling port."

"Is this a trap?" he asked quietly after absorbing her words, watching her closely.

Kat met his eyes. "Bree is my sister, my family. Drew is the only baby I've ever gotten close to, that I've ever loved. I would never hurt them. I'm doing this because I want them to be free. Bree loves you. She's not just contracted to you. That puts you in my sphere. And I'm thinking now, that there's a lot about you I'd like to get to know."

Danl grinned then and relaxed slightly. "We need to get going. We have a lot to do."

Bree finally spoke again. "Are the two of you insane? You can't really be serious."

"Yes," Kat said quietly. "I'm going and I want you with me. Bree, think about all the babies..."

Bree looked over at Danl, her fear evident. He nodded reassuringly and took her hand. Kat looked away, busying herself with Drew for a moment. She rose to take him over to a small grove of trees talking to him about what untamed trees looked like.

After a few moments, Bree and Danl joined them. Bree's eyes were bright with unshed tears, but she hugged Kat as Danl took Drew into his arms. Danl was the one that spoke. "I believe you, Kat. That you think this is the right thing to do. I don't understand, but I do believe you. You'll make sure Drew and Bree are safe." It wasn't quite a question, but Kat understood she needed to answer anyway.

"I swear on Gram's life." Still Bree searched her eyes, torn between their history together and this unbelievable request her friend was making.

Kat turned away then, there were still things to do. Time moved too quickly the rest of the day, but when it was time to leave for the shuttle, she moved rapidly to Lil's apartment. Lil let her in and Kat looked over her luggage. The medical pack was not in evidence and she looked over at Lil.

"I know I'm taking too much for just a couple of days, Kat, but indulge me." She opened her large piece and Kat saw the medical bag inside, taking up at least half of the room.

She smiled then. "Gramma, you can take anything you want. I'm here to carry it all." She looked over what Gramma was wearing and nodded. Her green boots were on her feet and she was wearing ods. Kat saw she had exercise pants underneath them. A larger thick shirt covered two regular shirts.

"We better get going. We have reservations, but you never know when some enforcer will come along and bump us." She grinned and took hold of the large pack. She was nervous, but excited and more than anxious to get back to Davd. She had to admit that to herself. It was a new feeling, but right.

Kat had Lil go ahead and take their seats, while she stayed with the luggage to see that everything was loaded. Head joined her at the luggage loading area.

"I'll see you after you get your family settled."

"Thank you. I'll be at the—"

"Don't wait for me. Go ahead with your plans."

"Yes sir," she said quickly, though unsure. This was Head; she'd do what he advised. The loader began moving and she watched the luggage go into the hold of the shuttle.

Head took a seat at the front of the shuttle, but Kat and Lil sat about half way back. She and Lil visited, talking about family, about how they didn't take enough time off as they observed the trees they were gliding over. At this height, they could see few details, but the land was obviously lush and fertile. That wasn't the kind of thing Kat had ever thought of on past trips, but a lot of things were changing at an extremely rapid pace for her now.

When they landed, she observed Head debark and move away with his large pack. She waited for their luggage then led Lil down to the food area.

Kat spotted Bree and her family and led Lil over to the table next to them. Lil managed to hide her surprise and played with the baby. "Have you eaten?" Kat asked.

"No, we've been waiting," Danl replied, while Bree looked away, refusing to meet Kat or Lil's eyes.

"Okay. Let's order. We have about twenty minutes, so you might want to get hand food."

They nodded and everyone got their meals. Kat used her gimp for everything, so that the others' presence wouldn't be overt. They gathered all of their packs and luggage together and ate at the table closest to the entrance to the recycling access she had used before. Head hadn't shown up, but she couldn't wait for him. It wouldn't be safe for the others. Besides, he had told her to go ahead. If anyone could look after himself, it would be Head, but she'd counted on his presence to keep the others reassured.

Kat's nerves were stretched tight, but Bree seemed to be coming apart with the waiting. Even Danl was becoming twitchy. Kat had also counted on Head to help them get their supplies down to the lower level, but they would make it somehow.

Kat looked around once more. Currently there was little traffic, which was one of the reasons for choosing this area. This was more of a lunchtime venue for eating, small tables and fast service to get back to the job quicker. This time of day, with fewer customers, serving was handled almost exclusively by machines.

She checked the time again then nodded to Danl. Bree slipped Drew into the harness pack she wore and picked up the smallest of their bags. Kat rose and took the handle of Lil's luggage. In the quiet, she heard the lock detach. The wall opened for the recycling bin. "Go," she whispered.

Gramma Lil went first carrying a smaller bag, then Bree with the baby, followed closely by Danl. Kat looked around one more time to make sure no one was observing them, then just before the wall slid back into place, slipped through herself.

The door had barely latched again when Kat heard Bree cry out in fear. She whirled, her weapon already out when she realized Head had joined them. He had his hands out, showing that he wasn't armed. Kat didn't lower her weapon. "Where did you come from?"

"I had a few things I needed to do and it's better that we didn't all enter at the same place."

"You're going with us?" It was Danl speaking. His voice was hard and cold with obvious distrust and more than a little fear.

"I am. Kat knows what's going on. There's a chance I've been compromised and I do not want anyone else put in danger because of me. I had to set up some new conduits and arrange my 'death'."

"What?" Lil spoke first.

"I need your gimps. That way if anything happens, we won't be easy to identify."

"Our gimps?" Bree responded, horrified. "No! We can't live without—"

"The gimp is just a monitoring device, Bree, but it has data that identifies you, your DNA. It doesn't hurt to be without it, I know. I'd been without mine for nearly a week until I came back for you."

The look on Bree's face told Kat what she thought about that. Kat removed her gimp and handed it to Head. Danl pulled his out as well. Lil needed a little help, but Kat removed it quickly. Danl reached for Drew and Bree pulled back, her look of betrayal was painful for Kat.

"Bree," Gramma Lil touched her arm. "It really is for the best and it can be replaced if it becomes necessary, look at Kat. Here, let me do it." Finally Drew and Bree's gimps were also in Head's hand. Kat could see that Head was impatient with the delay, but he said nothing.

"Come on, we need to get away from here. We're headed down. Let me carry that. I'll lead, Lil, behind me. Young man—"

"Danl, this is my wife, Bree."

Head nodded. "You walk in front of her, in case she loses her footing. These steps are only utilitarian. Lil, you and Bree be sure you hold on to the railing. Kat, you're at the end. Danl and I will carry the heaviest packs. Kat, keep your weapon out. I think we're ahead of things for now, but we need to take precautions."

Danl opened his mouth to argue, but looked over at Kat. She nodded her head to him and, after looking around, Danl began moving down the stairs loaded down with luggage. Head was carrying two large pieces of luggage, another strapped across his chest. Danl followed suit. Lil took a smaller pack so that she could hold on with one hand. Bree had the baby in his harness on her chest, one hand on him and the other on the railing. Kat draped the strap of the last piece over her head and held her weapon in one hand, the other lightly skimming along the rail. There was silence, but it wasn't hard to know what they were thinking, at least Danl and Bree.

Kat was purposely not thinking of how easy it had been to persuade Gramma Lil. There was something going on she still hadn't grasped, but it felt right. What they were doing was right.

Head called a halt after a couple of flights. Bree and Lil weren't used to this kind of activity and he and Danl were pretty loaded down.

As they were getting their breath, Head and Kat kept an eye out. They could hear no activity and after a short while, they continued on down. They moved slower this time, feeling more secure. Two more landings down, they paused again. They had barely set the luggage down when Bree screamed. Head's hand was over her mouth instantly, as Kat turned to face the danger with her weapon out.

"Davd!" She didn't get anything else out, because she was in his arms and his mouth was on hers.

Kat could see Bree goggling at them, but Gramma Lil only smiled. It was as though she'd been expecting this.

When they finally broke apart, he didn't take his eyes from hers and his hand caressed her hair. "It's been the longest fraking day of my life."

Her eyes sparkled with tears, but she laughed and leaned her head against him. "Me too," she whispered.

Finally he seemed able to release her and looked over at Head. "Good to see you, Ralt."

"I didn't think you'd noticed I was here," the man said dryly, then grinned and hugged his nephew.

"You just don't fit as well in my arms," Davd replied, then turned to the older woman. "You must be Lil."

She nodded and held out her hand. He ignored that and gave her a quick hug as well. He stepped back then and looked at the little family in front of him. Bree was still cringing back into Danl's chest.

"You must be Bree. I'm Davd. Kat has told me how important you are to her." He glanced down at Drew and smiled. Bree's arms tightened around the boy. "I think he's really going to enjoy where we're headed."

"Will he be safe?"

"You've brought Lil with you, as well as Kat and Head. I think so." He held out his hand again, to Danl.

"Davd."

"Danl," he responded and shook the ex-enforcer's hand.

"A couple more flights and you'll have a little time to rest. Ralt, Kat and I have to finish up some things, then we need to get moving. It shouldn't take long." He took the pack Kat had been carrying as well as Lil's. It was short work to reach the ground floor then. The packs were put down and Danl rubbed his shoulder. Kat and Davd turned to follow Head.

"You're going to leave us here?" Bree's voice was shrill now.

"No one knows we're here. This will keep us all safe," Davd assured her. "Rest, get your breath back. We shouldn't be long."

"Bree, I'm leaving Gramma Lil with you. You know I'll be back and that I consider this place very safe. Just sit and rest. Davd has already done most of the work."

"Go on," Danl said. "We'll be okay."

Kat nodded, gave Gramma Lil a quick hug, then she began jogging behind Ralt and Davd to the left.

Chapter Thirty-Three

They were soon out of sight and once again Kat was caught by how incredibly huge this place was. It just wasn't the kind of thing you seemed to be able to notice in the living areas, probably a critical design decision. After about twenty minutes at a good pace, they reached the area staged by Davd. Kat looked around in wonder. It did look as though a battle had been fought here. The area had scorch marks on the floor and walls. One of the handrails had been partially melted from a killing blast.

"We need a little blood now," Davd said. Ralt pulled a small container out of his pocket. It was full of a crimson fluid.

"Is that your blood?" Kat asked quickly.

Head nodded. "It was one of the things I had to take care of."

"I didn't—"

"We'll only need a drop or two of yours; just a prick of your finger. The incinerator is just back there. We'll have to leave a scrap of clothing caught in the handle. It's pretty obvious you would both put up a good struggle. Put your palm here, Kat, don't burn yourself. They'll be able to get DNA from it. With Head missing, there's going to be an incredible manhunt. I've left a nest over on the West side and this fight scene should cover us."

"I was able to reach Geof. He'll take over for us. It may take a while before normal communications are back up, but Geof will do a good job," Ralt reported to Davd. He took the container and splashed a bit of his blood near the stairs and more dribbling toward the incinerator.

Kat pricked her finger on her weapon and squeezed out a drop or two. She flung her hand out to scatter it toward the incinerator. With the next few drops, she allowed her blood to fall on the latch and let a button catch underneath it. She yanked her arm loose and she heard the fabric tear, leaving the button and a small piece of fabric behind. She then pulled a few hairs from her braid and stuck them to the corner of the door with blood. Head did the same with the corner of a stair, then all three stepped back to see the effect.

Kat turned to Head. "What do you think?"

"Looks good to me. It's our DNA, that wasn't faked at all. The scorch marks are from an enforcer's weapon. We're the only ones that have that high a setting."

Davd nodded. "We need to get back. Your friend is scared. I don't want to make it worse."

Kat looked around one more time, then they hurried back the way they had come.

As they neared the place they had left her friends, something caused Davd to slow down. He seemed to be listening intently to something and the hairs on the back of Kat's neck rose. He made some motion to Ralt and they both drew their weapons. Kat still hadn't heard whatever had alerted him.

Now with her heart thudding so loudly, she couldn't, but her weapon was also in her hand.

They veered off from their original trajectory, and at Ralt's signal, separated to approach from three different angles. Kat stifled a gasp as she finally got a glimpse of the scene. Danl was on the floor, unconscious or... Bree was kneeling beside him, Drew in her arms. It was his crying that Davd had heard, but it was tapering down to hiccups now. Cal had his hand around Gramma Lil's arm and his weapon trained on her.

Quickly and silently, Kat retreated and found Ralt. She reported her findings as he grimaced. "He always was a pain in the ass," Ralt muttered as Davd joined them.

"He has to know I'm here and probably Kat, but you may still be a surprise to him, Ralt. I think I need to go out there, get Lil released. He won't kill me, he wants to take me back and 'rehabilitate' me. That's always his goal."

"He'll know about me too. I was the one that purchased food while we waited for the recycler to open. I didn't want the other's IDs here."

"I have their gimps, so that should stump him for awhile," Ralt was thinking fast. So Kat kept quiet. "Look, you're right that he's going to know about both of you. Davd, you need to go out there, let him see you. If he asks about you, Kat, you'll have to do the same. Stay as far away from each other as you can, even if he orders you to move together."

Kat nodded, Cal wouldn't be able to hold a weapon on all three of them. Gramma Lil would need to remain calm. Kat had to force herself into professional mode. Everyone she loved was in terrible danger because of her and she had to save them. She felt Ralt's hand on her shoulder.

"I chose you because you're one of the best I've ever supervised. I've watched you for a long time and I know. Cal is a coward and no match for you or Davd. Keep it together, Kat."

She nodded and straightened her shoulders. Davd took her hand and squeezed it. "I'm not going to let anything happen to your Gramma. If he calls you out, check on Danl and stay away from me, keep him off balance."

Ralt nodded. "I'll be behind him. When he tells you to drop your weapons, do it. That will reassure him, especially if neither of you try to approach him."

"Danl—"

"Lil is staying calm for them, Kat," Davd said quietly. "I just don't think he's seriously hurt. Cal would have to take him out first. He could only handle a couple of women and a baby."

Kat forced a tight smile and nodded. "Let's go."

All three separated to approach Cal from different angles.

Davd stepped out, his weapon drawn. "Cal, let the woman go."

Kat saw Cal jerk slightly, very unenforcer-like, and turn to face Davd. The SOB kept Lil in front of him as a fraking shield! "Put your weapon down, Davd."

"Don't hurt the woman."

Cal pressed the stunner into Gramma Lil's side. "Your weapon. Put it on the floor, kick it over here."

Davd carefully placed his stunner on the floor in front of him. "Now, let the woman go, Cal."

"Where's the girl?"

Girl? Kat's eyebrow rose. Girl! The anger surprisingly steadied her. "The 'girl' is a trained enforcer, Cal." Kat smiled at Davd's tone. It sounded as though he were as offended at the description as she was.

"Where is she?"

"Here." Kat stepped out on the other side of Cal. That startled him and he jerked around.

"Weapon on the floor," he barked at her. She too laid her weapon down, but did not kick it toward him. "Get over there, with Davd."

Ignoring him now, Kat moved to Danl and knelt beside him. She felt for his pulse and found it, strong and steady. He'd only been stunned. She drew a breath and looked over at Bree. "Don't worry," she said quietly, hoping it sounded reassuring.

Bree sent a look of part relief, part fury at her, but kept quiet, holding Drew close. Kat rose and squeezed her shoulder. She glanced at Davd and gave him the tiniest of nods. He didn't acknowledge her, turning back to Cal.

"Let the woman go, Cal."

"Shut up, Davd! You've humiliated me. I'll probably lose my post for this. An enforcer, an enforcer that reports to *me,* turning shirker. Then the enforcer sent by *Head* shirks under my watch. I'm taking you both in, Puter can readjust you. Stand over there next to him," he demanded of Kat again.

"Let the woman go," Kat said quietly, ignoring his instructions.

Again Cal pressed the stunner into Gramma Lil's flesh and Kat knew she would be bruised tomorrow. "Do it. Secure his hands."

"Cal, just let us go. If we don't want to be here—"

"Puter can fix your psychosis. He can make you a productive member of society again."

"You sound like a program yourself. Just turn around and go back. Forget about us. If we die out there, your problem is solved and we won't be a burden on your 'society'." Davd kept talking, useless though it might be, giving Ralt all the time he needed.

"Maybe I should take care of that right now. An accident while capturing dangerous shirkers. You could be right, why waste the effort it would take to have you repaired." Cal moved the stunner up toward Lil's head and Bree whimpered in fear.

They all heard the sound of an especially strong blast and Gramma Lil swayed for a moment, then Cal fell to the floor, his grip on her going limp.

"Gramma!" Kat was moving before Cal hit the ground, her arms around her beloved grandmem.

"I'm okay. Kat, I'm okay. It wasn't me."

Ralt joined them then, kneeling to check on Cal. "He'll be out for awhile. How's Danl?"

Gramma Lil didn't answer, just going to his side. She too checked his pulse and his eyes. "He'll be fine, probably a headache, but it wasn't a full blast."

Kat thought Bree was going to drop Drew in her relief and she reached for the baby. "Get away from me!" Bree snarled at her, pulling away and Kat jerked back, her eyes wide.

Davd was beside her then and helped her to her feet, holding her against him.

"Bree, I—"

But Bree had turned away from her, placing her free hand on Danl's chest.

"Don't worry, Bree. He's fine, just sit here with him." Gramma Lil rose then and joined Kat, Davd and Ralt. "She'll be okay, Kitten. This has turned her world upside down and she's in shock. Give her a little time."

"I brought her because I wanted her to happy."

"And she will be. You made the right decision and her husband agrees."

Kat looked down at the still unconscious Danl. "Still?"

"Well, after the headache goes away," Gramma Lil managed to smile. "Now, what are we going to do about him?" She looked down at Cal.

Kat goggled at her. She had never, ever seen this side of her grandmem. She'd had no indication it even existed.

"Do you have anything that would help him forget about the last day or so?" Ralt asked.

Lil thought for a moment. "I think so, we don't use it often because of that side effect and I've never used it except for surgery, but this might be a good time. He won't feel very well when he wakes up."

"I feel terrible about that," Davd's sarcasm was strong and Kat thought for a moment he was going to kick the prone body, but he restrained himself.

"Let's take him to the scene we created. If he doesn't want to be humiliated by the fact that he let us all escape, let him be a hero instead. Let everyone decide that he captured us all and was injured while subduing us."

"And he threw all three of us in the incinerator?"

"Hey, if he's a hero, he can come up with the details for himself. There's no one here to dispute him," Ralt shrugged.

"It might work, especially with his ego. Come on." He and Ralt dragged Cal up and turned to head back to the incinerator.

"You're leaving us, again!" Bree's voice was hysterical.

"I can stay with—" Kat started.

"No! You're the cause of all of this. That man tried to kill Danl because you brought us to this—"

"Bree." Gramma Lil's voice was calm and sure. "Danl will be fine. I'll stay here with you while they make sure we're safe. Kat, why don't you leave a stunner with me, just to make her feel better?"

Kat looked over at Ralt, who nodded. For some reason this new surprise, that Gramma Lil knew how to handle a stunner, was less of a shock. Maybe after so many, everything felt less shocking.

Kat turned the stunner to strong stun and handed it to her. "We won't be long."

"Do what you have to do. Danl will be awake when you get back."

Kat nodded and hurried to catch up with the men. Davd looked over at her and took her hand. "You know Bree will forgive you for whatever she thinks is happening. You remember what it's like to shirk whether you want to or not, don't you?"

She looked up startled. Had her ideas turned so completely around so quickly? He was right. She had hated and despised him when she'd awakened out in a wilderness. And look at her now. She managed a nod and he winked at her.

Chapter Thirty-Four

It took little time to arrange Cal at the staged site. Ralt positioned his stunner just beside his hand and Davd had finally gotten the satisfaction of a few blows to his head and body. Hey, after a heroic fight like this man put up, he should have a few bruises, right?

They studied the scene, assuring themselves that it looked authentic, then jogged back to the others.

Danl was on his feet, though he looked a little the worse for wear when they returned. He was watching for them as Lil comforted Bree. They all sprang up when Danl motioned to them.

Davd drew them together. "There needs to be enough light to see, but hopefully not enough to be seen, when we get out of here." He took up some of the luggage and positioned himself behind Kat. He let himself caress her shoulder once, then they headed to the right.

They gathered around the door and waited.

"You've checked," Ralt spoke to Davd.

"Yes, it's how we came in this morning. I'll go first, just in case."

"What?" Bree asked, her voice at least an octave higher than usual.

"It's okay, Bree. Most of these doors have traps to ensure no one can exit, but this one is malfunctioning. I used it this morning. Please, trust me," Kat pleaded.

Bree didn't respond to that, just looking over at Danl. He nodded reassuringly and squeezed her hand. Kat was watching them and saw that Bree had several thousand questions for this man she had married and thought she knew. Instead she let her arms tighten around their son.

Davd moved to the door and glanced back at Kat. She nodded and he cracked the door open. There was no flash of light, no shock and he stepped outside.

"Is it dark enough?" She was beside him, to rescue him if necessary and his eyes locked on her face again.

"Yeah, in fact it's a little darker than I'd planned. You'll need to hold on to Lil and Bree. The ground is mostly level, but they'll need the support. Let Ralt, Danl and I carry everything. I'm going to let off one beam. When it's answered, you take the women directly to it. The wagons will be there waiting for you." He turned to the women then. "It's going to be colder than you're used to, but we'll get you wrapped up and in shelter as soon as possible. Pull your coat around the baby. He'll be warmer than the rest of us, next to your body. Please, try not to worry."

"Please," Kat repeated. "We have to move quickly. Would you like me to take Drew?"

"No!" Bree pulled away from her and Kat felt a stab of pain at the distrust in her face.

"Okay, you keep him, but let me take your arm."

Bree tensed, but allowed it. Gramma Lil gave Kat a reassuring squeeze of her other arm. They all stepped outside and Kat watched Davd signal toward the woods. One answering flash appeared and Kat fixed the area in her mind.

Kat placed her arm around Bree, feeling her tense and almost pull away, but Kat didn't let go. She took Gramma Lil's arm as well. "Did you see that light? That's where we're going. The land is firm and flat. Just stay with me and it'll take no time."

"Let's go, Kat," Gramma Lil urged her and they started off. Bree was reluctant, but after looking at Gramma Lil and back at Danl, she too moved forward.

Kat kept them at a steady pace, though she could feel them both shivering now from the cold.

"There, we've got 'em, Kat." A familiar voice sounded low out of the dark. "Bree, I knew you'd be along. Kat would never leave you behind."

"M-Mikeal?" Bree's teeth were chattering.

"Yes, it's me. Come on, get in the wagon. We can talk later." Mikeal helped her into the back of the wagon, then helped Lil in as well. "Lie down on the fur, you'll be warm soon."

Gramma Lil pulled Bree down beside her and Mikeal covered them both with another fur. Drew was watching with wide-eyed wonder at the night around him, apparently not the least bit concerned about the strangeness of everything. Kat saw tears in Bree's eyes but kept quiet. Hopefully Bree would come to understand and forgive her someday.

Kat turned back to help the men, but they had been right behind her and the bags were already being loaded onto the second wagon.

"Come on, we need to put some space between this place and us now," Davd said. Cal would be out for some time, but they might need every minute of it. Davd give Danl a hand into the seat of the wagon carrying Gramma Lil and Bree. Another fur was quickly wrapped around him as well. Davd looked over at Kat, who gave him a tremulous smile. He led her to the horses. His horse recognized her and whinnied, shoving his nose into her hand as she greeted him like an old friend. He must have been lonely today. Davd gave her a hand into the saddle.

Bree gasped at the sight of the huge animals and reached her hand out for Danl. "We're okay, Bree. Just stay under the fur, you'll be warm then. It's okay."

Gramma Lil took Bree's arm and pulled it down, covering them both up again, murmuring words that Kat couldn't hear.

Davd mounted behind her and she saw Head, she could think of him as Ralt now, take a horse just ahead of them. Mikeal and a man she didn't know had the wagons moving. They could talk later. There was only the light of the moons to guide them, but they made good progress and reached the camp set up for them in less than an hour.

The tents were already up and there was a small heating unit in each one. Kat led Bree, Danl and Drew to one of the tents and made sure they were as comfortable as possible. Bree had gotten warm under the furs with Gramma Lil and seemed too tired, from emotions as much as physical activity, to do more than crawl into the bag. Danl changed Drew's diaper and then joined her.

Kat joined Gramma Lil in their tent. "Is Davd joining us?" She asked, looking around.

Kat's face grew warm, not just from the heat of the unit. "Uh, no. He'll share a tent with Head, uh Ralt tonight."

Gramma Lil only nodded and crawled into her bag. She didn't, however, seem to be sleepy. "Kat, I think we need to talk."

"I had to do it, Gramma."

"What made you decide to shirk? I..."

Kat took a seat on her bag and tucked her feet inside. "I didn't."

"Now I really don't understand."

Kat sighed, but she owed Gramma Lil an explanation. The woman had just packed up and followed her without an argument. Kat had actually expected her to put up more of a fight than Bree, which was the total opposite of what had happened.

"I was sent to bring Davd back," she finally said. "Head sent me, telling me he was a shirker. He told me that since Davd was an enforcer, he needed someone he trusted to go after him. He told me I wouldn't be able to take him physically, that I'd have to outwit him. Well, you can see how that worked out. What I didn't know at the time was I was being set up. Ralt is Davd's uncle. I think he thought... I'd be good for the colony or something."

"I agree with him. Looks like he was right about sending you after Davd as well," Gramma Lil commented. Again Kat felt the color in her cheeks. Gramma Lil let her off the hook at that. "You never talked about shirking."

"I never planned to," Kat responded.

"Even after what Puter did to you?"

Kat blinked at that. "What?"

"Well, I knew how unhappy you were. I saw Mikeal at the wagon. I had lost track of him, but I still remember that day you both graduated. You were both distraught and, even if it is just my opinion, justifiably so. Puter telling Mikeal that he shouldn't be an engineer, when he was so obviously already a superb one." She sniffed. "The human educators were already talking about him. And as for you, to this day I haven't had an assistant—even one trained by Puter—half as good as you. Maybe you don't have the technical knowledge, but you have the instincts, the caring, that is essential for what I, for what *we* do. I am going to get to train you now, right?"

Kat's mouth had fallen open. "Will you?"

"Most certainly. I've never stopped wanting to."

"Gramma, I... I'm stunned. You never spoke of shirking. I was sure you'd be the one I had to convince, not Bree. But you've taken it so calmly. I admit, I don't understand."

"Tonight's not the time to get into it, Kat. Just know you've given me back a dream I had set aside a long time ago. I hope I can do the same for you. Come on, get in and keep me warm."

Kat crawled into the bag and in spite of everything racing through her head, fell asleep almost immediately.

She woke to the sound of the others beginning to break camp and woke Gramma Lil. "Hey, wake up. We need to get moving."

The older woman stretched, then smiled at her eager granddaughter. "I don't remember ever seeing you this happy."

Kat ducked her head, but was already pulling on her boots. "You'll be in the wagon again today, with Bree and Drew. I know we'd be home, uh, to the settlement tonight without the wagons. I don't know how much they will slow us down, but I'm glad we have them."

"Me too. I saw you riding on that horse last night. Very impressive."

"I got better," Kat laughed. She was still smiling when she emerged from the tent, to see Bree standing outside of her tent, shivering and angry as she watched it being dismantled. Kat hurried to her side. "Let's get you and Drew in the wagon, so you can cover up."

"What were you thinking! There's nothing out here, we're all going to die out here in the middle of nowhere!"

"Bree, please, calm down. I swear I would never—"

But Bree had turned away from her and Kat stared at her back. Danl joined them. "It's going to take her a little while, Kat."

"I want to go back! We can't live out here in this, this nothing!"

"No, Bree. Wait until you have all of the information before you make that kind of decision." Kat looked up at Danl, surprised. He was on her side? She had so much she needed to ask. For now though, she kept quiet, and watched Danl help Bree up into the wagon and tuck furs around her again. He handed her a cup of hot toa and a thick slice of bread. Gramma Lil moved past Kat, giving her a sympathetic look, and climbed up beside Bree. Gramma Lil thanked Danl for her cup and bread, and smiled at him.

He didn't even attempt to smile back. Gramma Lil kept quiet; there was already too much tension. She cuddled in next to Bree and the baby. The wagon started moving and she adjusted the fur up around Bree's neck.

"Have you nursed Drew this morning?"

Bree blinked at that. "I don't—"

"It's okay. Puter isn't paying attention out here. You have been nursing Drew, haven't you?"

After a moment, Bree nodded, blushing. "Just at night."

"Bree, it's a good thing. It's good for you and excellent for Drew."

"But I thought—"

"Puter told you differently. I know, but I'm the doctor, not Puter. Women have been nursing babies for thousands of cycles. Nursing gives the baby your immunity. How do you think babies lived in the dark ages, before there was medicine and incredible doctors like me?" Gramma Lil winked at her.

"I don't have any milk right now. I only nurse at night."

"Nurse now anyway, nurse every chance you get. Your milk will come back and you'll start producing enough to satisfy him in no time."

"Really?"

"Ask Kat, she's studied enough of my discs."

Instead, Bree turned away, but did bring Drew to her breast. The baby was completely covered but Gramma Lil watched Bree's face, knowing when her milk let down. Rather than an "I told you so," Gramma Lil smiled and returned to looking around at the landscape. She winked at Kat who had heard the entire conversation.

In moments, all sign of the camp were gone and they were moving again. Kat was once again sharing a horse with Davd, while Ralt rode the horse she had ridden out from the village. In the daylight she could see how accomplished a horseman Ralt was, and wondered when he had gotten the practice.

They had been riding an hour or so when Davd nuzzled her ear. "You remember the problem I had last time we rode like this?"

"Shh!" she hissed at him, her face hot.

"I've got the same problem now."

"Davd!" she was whispering, but he could hear her fine.

"It's crowded out here today. I liked our last trip better."

"You miss your pet liger?"

He chuckled then and his arm drew her even closer. "Warm enough?"

"Almost too warm, thank you."

"Hey, me too." She laughed out loud then. Neither noticed the looks they received from Ralt and Gramma Lil. "When we get home, you can have a nice hot bath so you won't be putting those cold feet on me."

"Will I be, uh, living with you?"

"Uh, yeah, if you want—"

"What about Gramma Lil?"

"Do you want her to live with us?"

Kat blinked at that. She would be living with Davd? They had made no formal arrangements, no contract. They hadn't even discussed it. "Where else could she live?"

"With Carla, next door. They're about the same age, they might even know some of the same people, you know?"

"Will Carla mind?" Kat asked anxiously. She shouldn't have just assumed she and Gramma Lil would qualify for a house.

"No. It was her suggestion when I told her we were going to try to bring Lil back here."

Kat nodded but didn't speak. He had made arrangements for her gramma before they left the village? That spoke of a commitment they hadn't discussed, didn't it? Rather than have such a discussion in public, riding as they were on the horse, she kept quiet.

His arm tightened around her waist and he murmured in her ear. "May I join you in the bath?"

"That might be nice," she whispered and he placed a light kiss on the back of her neck.

Chapter Thirty-Five

Dark was falling fast by the time Kat spotted signs of the village. She'd begun to worry what another night in a tent would do to Bree, so she breathed a sigh of relief.

Men from the village met them and quickly took charge of the horses. Kat spotted Gart speaking with Ralt, then Gart moved to help Bree and Gramma Lil down from the wagon. He bent over to speak to both women. Kat started to move in their direction, but Davd stopped her.

"Let him welcome them. He can escort Bree and Danl to their new home. It's part tradition, part reassurance for Bree."

"What about Gramma Lil?"

"Carla already has her, see?"

As Kat watched, Gramma Lil started walking beside Carla, talking animatedly about something Kat couldn't hear. She did remember at the last minute to turn and wave at Kat, then she disappeared into Carla's home. Well, she certainly seemed to be fitting in well.

Kat turned to see Gart help Bree up the stairs to a house a couple of structures down from Davd's. It was bigger than his and she could see the smoke coming from the chimney.

"Will she be okay?"

"I think so. They warmed up the place and filled the boiler before we arrived. She needs a little time." Davd tried to reassure her.

"I know, I just didn't expect her to..."

Davd dismounted and lifted her off the horse. He held her for a minute, then waved to Ralt and turned her toward his house.

"What about Ralt?"

"Don't worry. Everyone is taken care of. He'll probably sleep in one of the rooms in the dining hall for now. Then he can decide for himself. If you have to worry about someone, make it me this time. Will we both fit in the tub?"

She chuckled, but allowed him to lead her inside. The fire had indeed been laid and the cabin was nicely warm.

"Warm up. I'll start the bath."

She smiled and moved closer to the stove.

In a few minutes she heard him. "Hey, Kat!"

She turned with a smile on her face and joined him in the bathroom. He was already sitting in the tub, leaning back, his arms crossed behind his head. She looked at him, trying not to smile. He thrust slightly toward her and she chuckled.

"I'm not going to get very clean, am I?"

"No, ma'am. You are not, but I think you will be warm."

Well, he'd been right about that. She was very warm when he bundled her into the bed. She didn't even need the robe, tucked up against the warmth radiating from his body.

Chapter Thirty-Six

A knock on the door of the cabin woke them both the next morning. Davd looked over at her, but took the robe out of her hand. "This messes up my plans," he whispered and headed out to the main room.

"Uh, sorry to disturb you," Ralt's voice caused her to duck completely under the covers. She needed to get some more clothing. "Gart wants us all to meet at his office to debrief."

"Sure, we'll be there in a few minutes." He said something else, but Kat didn't hear it.

Gart had invited them all into his office instead of going to the large dining area. It was crowded but he'd had breakfast brought in for them. Kat was a little surprised to see Bree there, but gave her a small smile. Bree only looked worried cuddling Drew tighter. She looked away when she saw Kat.

"I know you're not all settled in, but I thought a brief history lesson about this place might be in order." Gart said. "I know now that some of you were unaware of us, but we're not a new village. This place was settled over forty cycles ago. While Thirdport was being constructed, several of the couples became concerned that no true colonization had begun. By that time, Centerport was nearly ten cycles old and Secondport was six or seven, yet everyone was still 'inside.'

"A small group, well, I guess you would say they mutinied and slipped away to find a place to settle. There were just a few of us then, I was only a child, but we had good contacts at the arcologies, and a lot of assistance making the plans. Some people stayed behind as conduits at Thirdport and eventually at the other two ports. The people who moved to this village permanently were listed as victims of accidents by those contacts, so no one searched for them. I guess it would be accurate to say we stole from the colony. We took the equipment to thaw the horses and other livestock. We took other machines that were unnecessary in the boxes, but necessary for life outside. Things that obviously weren't going to be used anywhere else. These technologies and equipment were shipped here for our use. Finally someone was going to use them. It was easier with a new port, accidents do happen. The people at the first two ports didn't realize that the opportunity would never be there for a legitimate 'escape'. This is the oldest village on the planet, but not the only one.

"Ralt and his father, Elt, had been helping us since before Chi died, but it was slow going, making sure Puter didn't discover us." He smiled at Kat's gasp. "Yes, Chi was definitely a part of this settlement. It was his dream as well and he wanted his family to grow and flourish here, not die out after only three generations. Everything was on paper, nothing on-line and we have those original plans in our archive." He looked over at Bree for a moment. "Someday we'll want our ancestors to know what we went through, what we accomplished."

"You knew Chi?" Gramma Lil asked.

"He's the main reason we're here, Lil. I know he planned to tell you everything, but..."
****

Chi rubbed his forehead in an unconscious manner. What the frak had he stumbled onto? This was old code, encoded into Puter before his parents had ever left Rth. No one would have found this without a deep search; that's how he'd found it. Even with his skills, he'd almost missed it. This was definitely not what he'd been searching for. It had just never occurred to him.

It was his own ego; he recognized that now. He'd wanted to discover why he and Lil were only to have one grandchild. He knew of no genetic problem, surely Lil would have found it if there was one. There was nothing wrong with Castra, she was beautiful, intelligent and healthy, yet she would have no children. Patik was allowed only one—Kat. In spite of his worry, even the thought of his little kitten brought a smile to Chi's tired face.

She was a treasure, so bright, so much fun to be around already. She was already reading, and loved listening to his and Lil's stories of old Rth, passed down from their parents.

So his ego had overcome him and he'd decided to check on why she would have no siblings or cousins.

He'd never thought to find something like this.

Someone had sabotaged Puter and they'd done it before anyone had ever left Rth. The code he'd discovered wasn't that sophisticated, maybe that's why he had spotted it, but it had been fraking well hidden and protected.

One of the environmentalist groups? A radical splinter group at least, to have decided to doom an entire space colony. And doom was the long-term effect of this program.

If he had interpreted it correctly, and he was good at what he did, Puter was already on task for decreasing the population. There would never be the true colonization that his ancestors had foreseen. There was no plan to *ever* leave the arcologies.

Whoever had hidden this program deep within Puter ensured that this planet would never be "harmed" by humans. Obviously, they'd had no confidence that humans could learn from their mistakes. The technology to live in harmony with this planet was available now. The arcologies themselves were proof of that, weren't they? No pollution went into the environment, thousands of people in such a small space and the atmosphere, the land, everything was clean, pristine as though they hadn't arrived. Which had been the saboteurs' goal, though not in the same way. The difference was, the colonists and their children had learned to inhabit a planet and still not destroy it.

How short sighted! This would have to be corrected. He probably could extract the program, but not before he consulted some of his friends who felt the same. Yes, he needed to talk to his friends about it first. As he abhorred the actions of some sort of fanatics working in secret, without the knowledge or wisdom of the people they were affecting, he would not do the same.

He must talk to his "co-conspirators." He wasn't alone in wondering why they were still in these boxes after all this time. He was aware of plans being drawn up to set up a third village, like the secret one near Thirdport, he was assisting in the effort. It was well past time. He'd lived on this planet long enough to have a grandchild and they were still inhabiting basically none of the planet. The people from Thirdport had the right idea.

****

Chi arrived at Elt's apartment without warning. It was safer for everyone that way. Elt and Cara were home and greeted him warmly.

"You may not be so happy to see me once I explain why I'm here," he accepted a cup of toa from Cara.

"Does it have anything to do with the project? Is there a problem?" Elt asked quickly.

"Yes and no," Chi sighed. "I know why we're still in the boxes. We're here forever."

"What?" Cara took a seat beside Elt. "You can't be serious."

Chi nodded. "I found a program, an old one, by accident this afternoon. I don't know how to... Puter won't be letting us out and the population will continue to shrink."

"Why?"

"I can't imagine what they were thinking. It would have been simpler to blow the space ships up in orbit instead of this slow death they planned." He waved his hand and put the cup down. "A program was installed that will gradually cause the colony to die out without ever leaving the boxes. That's why the decrease in population. Whoever did this planned it carefully. We rely on Puter for everything and very few people question it. Everyone refers to Puter as 'him' now, as though it were a personality, a higher being."

They sat there in shock. Cara jumped when the door opened and their son Ralt and daughter Lia enter. Lia excused herself and went to her room. Ralt took a seat, noting their serious expressions. He was studying to be an enforcer and Puter determined that he would not be reproducing. That was part of why Elt and Chi had started talking.

Chi looked at Elt for a clue whether or not to continue, but Elt turned to Ralt. "I trust you, son, but what we're talking about could put you in danger. Not to mention ourselves. If you stay, I need your word you will not discuss this with anyone. What we're discussing could be considered treason to Puter." After another look at Chi, Elt brought the young man up to date.

"It doesn't sound like treason, Da," Ralt said quietly, after listening to the whole discovery. "We came here to live all over the planet, not just in these arcologies. I've read the history—"

"You've read the *family* history. I know that's not what they teach you in school."

Ralt smiled. "True, but I feel like I'm more educated because of it. I don't think building small settlements near the arcologies would be bad for the planet. We could use the technology we've developed to ensure we don't pollute anything. If the settlements are close, they can be monitored to ensure that we're not doing any harm."

Chi smiled. "That's exactly what I'm talking about. Except for the monitoring, that's precisely what they did at Thirdport. We need to take it slow of course, but not generations slow like we have been. And we do need a larger population. If I take this programming out... " He looked over at Elt.

Elt nodded. "Yes, we came here to grow into this planet. I honestly don't know anyone to consult about this. There are so few of us working on it. Puter's programming hasn't really needed upgrading since our arrival. In most areas there's been no reason. The project on Rth was thorough, trying to think ahead for any contingency. But if our projections are correct," he glanced down at his notes, scribbled on paper, not his pad, "this colony is going to be dying out in less than six generations. I'll be gone, but I certainly want my genes to continue here. My parents came here for that purpose and I happen to agree with it." He grinned at Ralt and winked.

Ralt chuckled and looked over at Chi. "If I don't have a kid or two, he'll never get over it."

"I certainly understand that," Chi nodded. "If I can take the programming out, you can probably have a dozen if you want."

"Uh, thanks?" Ralt said causing both men to laugh out loud.

"There's one more thing." Chi cleared his throat. This hit as close to home as the first revelation. "You know on Rth living to be 90 cycles old wasn't unheard of, but here seventy is about max. That's not because of genetics, my friends."

"You think Puter is... is getting rid of the older generation?" It was Cara who voiced the question.

"I do. Puter is squeezing the population from both ends. It's been subtle, but it's being done. I want to talk to Lil about it, bring her into this. I want to know if anything is being introduced into our gimps after we reach a certain age. I'm talking something slow acting, but eventually lethal."

"Chi—"

"I know, I'm getting paranoid now, but the more I look into the programming, the more I believe it's possible. Whoever did this, did not want this colonization to happen. As of now, they're winning."

"Talk to Lil, Chi. She needs to be part of this." Chi nodded and after apologizing for ruining their evening, he left them.

Headed home, he made up his mind to talk to Lil. The time for protecting her from this knowledge was past. He stepped inside to find Patik and Keira there with Kat. He would not spoil their time with Kat. While he knew that Patik would agree, there was a bit of rebel in his son, he would not discuss this in front of Keira. Instead he pulled Kat onto his knee and tickled her, reveling in the sparkle of her laugh. Yes, she alone was reason enough to take on this task. Shortly Lil was called out for an emergency. At Kat's bedtime, Patik picked her up. "She'll be asleep before we get home." He smiled down indulgently as his daughter and shared a chuckle with Chi.

He sat down to wait for Lil, but she pinged him that she would be late, so he'd gone on to bed. Asleep when she returned, there had been no time to discuss something of this magnitude with her the next morning.

He felt a deadline looming over them on this, one that he couldn't shake. No one knew what he'd been investigating, they couldn't know, but the sense of urgency did not abate. He shoved that aside. Both Patik and Castra were young enough to have children, more children, Ralt as well.

He went to work as usual and hurried to finish so that he could explore the unfamiliar coding of the older program.

****

Chi finished his meal and burped discreetly. In some cultures, it was a compliment. Lil didn't feel that way. He was tired, and he didn't want to go back, didn't want to face that protected program that meant their doom. But who else was there? He needed to get to the bottom of this discovery. Immediately his mood darkened. It was crucial, but it was much more complicated than even he'd first thought. There seemed to be safeguards around the program and he was moving much more slowly than he'd anticipated. He still hadn't found the right time to discuss this with Lil, but he wouldn't allow himself to be caught up in the work tonight. He'd come home at a decent hour and they would have that discussion.

"You okay?" Lil touched his shoulder.

"Yeah, just thinking."

"That's not usually hard for you. Can I help?"

"You do, just being here."

Her brow furrowed then. "Chi, what is it?"

"Just work," he demurred. He needed to think about this. He did plan to tell her, he knew she felt the same way and she wanted more grandchildren. She felt Castra's ache as though it were her own. He hadn't wanted to put her in a position of having to feel conflict with Puter, not yet anyway. No, that was backward thinking. They needed to be in open rebellion soon, it was time to admit that. But, he was no longer as confident that the program could be removed so easily or so discreetly. If he didn't know better, he'd think Puter had... encompassed the program.

The tag he'd discovered just this afternoon needed to be investigated carefully. He found that he was reassuring himself that Puter was only wires and circuits, not a maleficent entity. His stomach clenched at the thought.

He made his decision and stood. "I need to go back to work."

"Now?" Lil said, concerning coloring her voice.

"I won't be late. There're just a few things I'm checking into and I need to do it now, while it's fresh on my mind and there are fewer distractions."

"Want some company?"

He chuckled then, sounding much more like himself. "Did I just say I needed *less* distractions? Besides, you'd be bored to tears. I won't be long."

He leaned down and kissed her, then took up his pack and left their apartment.

Never to be seen alive again.

A massive heart attack while he sat at his desk. It made no sense, there was no history of heart problems in his genetic makeup, but they refused Lil permission to do an examination and to be honest she wasn't sure she could.

Chapter Thirty-Seven

Lil sat staring at Ralt, her eyes shining with unshed tears. "Why didn't you tell me?"

"We didn't feel like we could tell anyone. The decision was made that you would be safer this way. We had to be so careful after Chi was murdered."

"M-murdered?" Bree was the one that finally spoke. "You're accusing Puter of murder?"

"Yes," Ralt said quietly. "It took me cycles to see the autopsy that Puter had done on Chi. It was a joke. Even I could have done a better job. In fact, if you checked, and I'm sure you couldn't, you'd find that one wasn't really done."

"Was Da killed as well?" Kat's voice sounded breathless and Davd's arm went around her.

"We immediately started an investigation after his death. The accident made no sense, but we weren't able to find any reason other than he was Chi's son."

"He was doing code," she said softly.

"What?" Ralt and Gart sat up straight, staring at her in shock.

"It was his secret. He was working with a friend, because programming was what he had always wanted to do, like I always wanted to be a doctor. Grandda taught him, kind of like you taught me." Kat looked at Gramma Lil. "Da knew Grandda's work, he would have recognized it."

"When did he tell you this?" Gramma Lil asked.

"Just a few days before... "

"I never... he never told me."

"No, it was our secret. But if he was just doing code—"

"He must have found something Chi left behind, something he would recognize, a marker of some kind. That would have made him want to dig deeper." Ralt was talking to Gart now, shaking his head. "We didn't talk to him about this. We thought we were protecting the rest of the family. Lil... " Gart looked over at Gramma Lil. "I'm so sorry."

She shook her head. "It's what Chi would have done. He never spoke of this, even to me. He was trying to protect us as well. If he could have removed the program..." She shook her head. "I knew he always wanted to move on, out of the arcologies and on to the planet," she sighed. "That's how Kat was able to talk me into this so easily. We'd always dreamed it would happen in our lifetimes. When Kat was the one that came to me..." She smiled and took her granddaughter's hand. "Thank you."

"Gramma, I wish—"

"Shh, we're here, you've made Chi's dream come true for me."

Suddenly Kat went stiff, "Castra."

Lil met her eyes. "That's why she was sent to Thirdport to complete her training. It never made sense. Puter didn't want her near Chi's work."

They both turned to Ralt. "Slow down. She's safe. She has been for cycles. If we bring anyone else connected to you out here now, it will endanger us all."

After a moment Kat nodded. "You're right." She took Lil into her arms.

They had matching tears in their eyes.

Chapter Thirty-Eight

Kat lay in that space between waking and sleep, semi-aware that a large warm hand was caressing her. She roused herself and rolled toward him when they both heard the knock on the door. He collapsed back onto the mattress. "I'm getting a fraking lock," he muttered before the second knock, then the sound of the door opening.

"Kat?"

"Gramma? Are you okay?"

"I'm fine. Get dressed right now. You're going to deliver a baby."

Kat blinked, wide-awake now.

"Hurry, I'm going on over," Gramma Lil said as the door shut behind her.

Kat was already scrambling into her clothes. A baby? Good Galt!

Davd stayed where he was, watching her. The excitement in her eyes and the color in her cheeks made her almost as beautiful as when they made love.

"I don't know how long this will take—" She started as she turned toward the door.

He caught her hand and drew her back to the bed for an instant. He sat up and pulled her down, kissing her nose. She laughed then and he watched her mesmerized.

"I'll find something to do, but I miss you already." He kissed her lips then and she responded, but immediately pulled back.

"Later," she whispered and was gone.

He lay back against the pillow for a moment. She was off to deliver a baby. There would probably be a great deal of practice around that here. He'd never given it that much thought. He'd known since he was ten that he was obligated by Puter to have one son. The way his life had been then, he had shoved the information aside. When he had realized the leverage it had given him with women, as he grew older, he had to admit he'd used it, at first. After he learned what pleased women he had again pushed the thought away.

He'd never wanted to bring a child into the world in some sort of short-term contract, to live the life he'd had, so it was shelved. Hadn't he vowed, as just a kid, to never allow that to happen? He'd reconciled himself to just that, but now, out from under Puter for good...

Why was the image of Kat, holding a child so intriguing? Not his typical daydream. That was for sure. They were together right now, yes, but they'd not yet discussed any future. He'd said he wanted a conversation as soon as they arrived back here, but so much happened so quickly and this was not a quick conversation he wanted.

Kat was so different from any woman he'd been with before. The word that kept coming back to him was "real." No enhancements, no pretending during sex, true love for her family and friends. All of that was rare in his experience and he liked every bit of it. He was going to make time for their talk, maybe after dinner tonight, if she was free.

He rose and dressed then headed for the stables. The horses knew her and liked her. He could discuss it with them. He smiled at the thought.

Chapter Thirty-Nine

It was indeed Dana in labor as Kat entered the delivery room of the infirmary. She smiled over at Kat. "Told you there would be a lot of practice," she said.

"You two know each other?" Gramma Lil asked, looking at Kat.

"The first night," Kat replied, "when I saw all of children. I thought you'd be next."

Dana chuckled, then went silent and closed her eyes, breathing shallowly. The man at her side took her hand and she squeezed. Kat looked over at Gramma Lil. "She's doing very well. It's her third, so she'd on top of things."

"Third," Kat said almost reverently. She knew no one who'd given birth to three children. Two was the maximum inside. "Inside," she thought the word with some amusement. Her life really had shifted 180° if she thought of the arcologies that way.

Dana blew out a breath, then took a long cleansing breath. "I don't think it's going to be long," she spoke to the room, but look up with adoring eyes at the man beside her. "Kat, this is Will, my husband."

Husband? They used that term here, not partner. Just the sound made Kat feel warm. They shook hands, then Gramma Lil nodded toward the counter. "Go ahead and seal up. You need to check her dilation."

Kat nodded, at least pretending competence. Gramma Lil was here. She sealed her hands with the spray. For just an instant the thought came that this should be added to her pack, then she remembered. Now was not the time to think of any infection she might have given Davd. It hadn't happened, focus.

Following Gramma Lil's whispered instructions, she waited until the next contraction ended, then made her quick, gentle as possible, measurement.

"Has your water broken?" Kat asked Dana, who nodded. Kat turned to Gramma Lil. "She's almost crowning and at ten."

"You felt the baby's head?"

Kat nodded, the wonder taking her voice for an instant.

"She's been having contractions off and on for a few days, but nothing steady. I brought her over as soon as her water broke," Will spoke quietly as well.

Gramma Lil nodded and looked over at Kat, who squared her shoulders and took a deep breath. "Will, why don't you go ahead and get in place? Dana, I need you to give me a small push with the next contraction."

Dana nodded and when it began, braced herself against Will's chest, her feet against the blocks at the end of the table and pushed. Kat smiled and watched as the baby receded into Dana's body when the push ended.

"The baby's right here, Dana. A couple more and you'll be enjoying the fun part."

Gramma Lil looked over at Kat in surprise. That was exactly the right thing to say, where had she learned it? That was for later. Gramma Lil relaxed though, Kat was instinctively a doctor. Of course, there had never been any doubt in her mind.

In two pushes the head was out. Kat felt quickly for the cord, then nodded to Dana. "You're doing great. Give me a big push now."

That was all it took. The baby all but tumbled into Kat's calm, firm hold and howled her fury. Kat laughed, sucking out her nose and mouth, then lay the infant on Dana's stomach. "I didn't like outside too much myself when I first saw it. I think you'll come to like it fine though." She clamped the cord and Will quickly cut it.

"Her name's Katy. We didn't know you when we chose it, but it fits even better now," Dana said taking the baby to her breast.

Kat blinked, then turned back to her duties, not sure what to say to that anyway. The placenta was delivered easily and placed in quick storage to be preserved for later.

Gramma Lil and Kat stepped aside for a moment to give the little family time to bond. "You were wonderful," Gramma Lil looked up at Kat.

"Promise me they'll all be that easy."

"I wish I could, but to have one so successful under your belt first will definitely help. We need to take her and check her out. Looks like she's nursing well."

The exam showed a healthy baby girl and mem. They left the three of them alone then, with a young woman to act as runner if one was needed. The two of them headed to the main building to get some breakfast. Kat assured Will they would be back soon and in any case were less than twenty-five running strides away. Dana assured them that was fine and shook her head indulgently at Will as they left.

They were practically assaulted as they entered the dining room. Gramma Lil stepped back to let Kat make the announcement of the birth of Katy. Kat saw Lil's grin, and realized she was blushing at the applause.

Kat looked around for Davd, but he wasn't there. He'd probably eaten earlier and gone somewhere to work. As far as she knew he still didn't have a permanent assignment, but that wouldn't keep him idle. She and Gramma Lil visited with the people at their table, the woman who would probably deliver next was there, and introduced herself. Bess still had a few weeks before her second child was due.

Kat spotted Bree come to the door and hesitate. Before she could wave her over, the other woman had turned away and let some women with children the same age as Drew draw her to their table. Kat returned to her food, and tried to ignore Gramma Lil's look of sympathy.

Mikeal came in and spotted her, with only Gramma Lil beside her, and approached. "I heard about the new baby. Congratulations."

"It's Dana and Will that deserve congratulations," Kat reminded him.

"Not for that, for getting to be a doctor."

Kat's smile grew. This was someone who fully understood, maybe even better than Bree. He'd lived the trauma himself. It was time to return to the infirmary for another check. That was only prudent, so she rose.

"Go ahead, Kat. I'll be there in a few minutes," Gramma Lil said and turned back to Bess.

Kat fell into step beside Mikeal. "I didn't have time to ask before. What are you doing now, if not agriculture?"

He grimaced and she laughed he walked her toward the infirmary. "Actually, I am doing some agriculture, teaching it anyway. I was well trained, if unhappy. My main job is checking on the equipment, machining parts as spares before the old ones wear out. Some of the equipment we have here is your Grandmem's age, so it's time to check everything out."

They visited for a few minutes, then she told him goodbye and he squeezed her hand, which surprised her a little. She stepped inside and found everyone doing well. Dana was asleep, so Kat took Katy into her arms to examine her more closely. It did feel good to hold the child, to know that she had a part in her well being.

For the first time ever, Kat found a slight longing in her for this experience. She did love Drew. She had from the moment she'd first held him, when he was mere minutes old, but this little girl had known her touch from before her birth. Out here, the possibility of a child was really there for her. She blushed when she realized that the face of the man hovering protectively over her, as Will had done, was Davd.

They hadn't discussed anything of the sort. Of course they hadn't really had time. Could he want something like this with her? She'd vowed never to contract, but that's not what happened here. The couples here were like Gramma Lil and Grandda Chi, committed to each other.

She was being foolish; she'd known Davd for a little over a week.

****

Davd had finished mucking out the stalls. It wasn't his duty, but it had to be done, so until he did get an assignment, he might as well help. His thoughts kept drifting back to Kat. Was everything going well with the delivery? He'd found himself staring over at the infirmary more than once, but there was no way he could go over there.

His daydream from earlier returned. Kat holding their child. It didn't seem so very far-fetched when he really thought about it. He'd vowed never to contract, never to have the child that Puter had decreed for him, but that was before. Had he really only know Kat for a week?

Again he found himself starting to head in the general direction of the infirmary when he saw the door to the main building open and sound of Kat's laugh came to his ears. He looked that way in anticipation and was surprised to see Mikeal hold the door for her and that her laughter was for something he'd obviously said. Why the fratz did that cause his chest to feel tight? She'd be rousted from *his* bed this morning.

He didn't step farther out of the shadow of the stable door, but continued to watch and heard himself hiss when Mikeal took her hand for an instant before she stepped inside and out of his view. It looked, at least from this viewpoint, like the man had started to lean in and... Mikeal stood there, watching the door though which she'd disappeared for a moment, before turning away.

Davd turned away as well and resumed his work in utter silence. He felt the shove from behind and turned to see the horse that had carried the two of them after her horse had been killed and again when they had returned here to live. It whinnied at him and shoved him with his nose again as though to push him out of the stable. Davd absently patted the horse's nose, but didn't speak, finishing up his work. He avoided the dining hall. In truth he avoided everything after that, taking some tack outside to clean. He needed the mindlessness of it.
****

Kat returned to the house she considered home after her check on Katy and Dana, but there was no sign of Davd. She missed him and wanted to share her morning with him. No reason not to admit it. It wasn't just the sex, he was right about her body being set free, but it was him that had done that, and only him that she wanted. She felt foolish even thinking that but there it was. As an enforcer, okay ex-enforcer, she knew to trust the evidence.

He was out working and she should be as well. If nothing as exciting as delivering a baby, there were often small injuries coming in according to Marm. Davd could find her there easily enough.

He didn't though and she found herself having dinner with Marm and some of the other women. It wasn't so very uncomfortable. These women wanted to get to know her and were very welcoming, but what kind of assignment had he taken for today?

After a final check on "her" little family, and accompanying them back to their own home, she returned to hers to find him sitting at the table, his back to the door.

"Davd! I was looking for you."

"Did everything go all right?"

The words were right, but his tone was off, flat somehow. "It went perfectly. There's a new baby girl here and she's healthy and it was—" She just threw her hands into the air. "I was a doctor! Of course Gramma was there, but she let me handle it. Oh Davd, it was better than I'd ever dreamed. I was a real doctor."

"I guess just fixing up my shoulder didn't compare."

Something was definitely not right, but she wasn't sure how to respond. "I didn't have to turn anything to ash afterward this time," she finally offered.

"Yeah," was his only comment.

"Did you eat?"

"Not hungry."

She stepped closer now, all of the joy of her day draining away and fear seeping in to replace it. "Is something wrong?"

"So was that your whole day? Anything else happen?"

"Uh, not really. I pulled a splinter out of a little boy's hand. I don't remember his name. The one with the blonde hair that keeps falling into his eyes."

"So that's all?"

"Davd," her voice trembled on the word. "What happened? Did I do something..."

He finally faced her then and his eyes seemed more sad than angry. He shook his head and rose. "I'm tired. I took a bath already, worked in the stables today. I'm going on to bed."

She watched him walk past her without touching her hand or shoulder and she felt cold to her marrow. With a courage that stunned her, she grabbed his arm. "What did I do? Talk to me, please."

He stopped. "Talk to you, that was my plan tonight. I wanted to finally have that conversation I mentioned before we went back for Lil and the others."

"But now you don't want that?"

"We don't really know each other that well. There're lots of things about me you don't know and I'm sure there are things you haven't shared with me."

More puzzled and confused than ever, she met his eyes. "You know more about me than anyone on the planet except Gramma and Bree. You know things about me that they don't even know."

He took a breath and the words seemed to wrench out of him. "Do you want to tell me about Mikeal?"

"Who? Mi-Mikeal? The one who are assigned agriculture by Puter?"

"The man who hugged you when we first arrived."

"I don't know anything about him to tell you. I lost track of him when we all went into training. I never even knew he'd shirked."

"But you're close with him. You knew him in school, were friends."

She shook her head in bewilderment. "Close to him? I've had maybe three conversations with him in my whole life. Why are you asking about him?"

"You were with him today, laughing and holding hands. I thought he was going to kiss you."

"What are you talking about?"

Her obvious confusion got through to him that time. "I saw you. You were coming out of the main building, you were laughing with him and he took your hand."

It took her a moment, then she faced him. "Yes, I did see him today. It was right after Katy was born. I got a bite to eat and went back to check on her and Dana. I think he was there but I have no memory of holding his hand and he most certainly wasn't about to kiss me." Now indignation tinged her voice.

"He wanted to," Davd shot back.

"I don't care, even if he did." She rose up then and met his lips with her own. Galt, how many firsts could one day hold?

Instantly his arms were around her, pulling her to him. Her arms were around his neck bringing her even closer if that were possible.

A long time later, when they broke the kiss, it was to find her legs around his waist and one of his hands deeply entangled in what was left of her braid. "He's not important to you?" Davd growled.

"Who?" she managed to say before his lips took hers again.

"Are you mine?"

"If you'll have me. Are you mine?" she asked, looking into those beautiful eyes.

"Yes. I've been waiting for you."

The Beginning

Rth Claimed, the second in this series will be available soon – here's a snippet for you

Rth Claimed
Chapter One

Torr Franks stepped into his apartment and stopped dead. Part of the reason was there was no room to move. The other was that the obstructions all seemed to be Enforcers. That couldn't be good. He spotted his mate Castra on the couch, looking harassed and worried. He shoved his way through. "What's wrong?"

"I don't..." she stopped as the small man who seemed to think himself in charge stepped forward blocking Torr's path.

"27226TRF?"

"Yes. Who are—"

"Are you contracted to 29181CCS?"

Torr looked down at Castra. "I am. Who the frak are you?" His patience gone now but anger was taking its place.

"Head of the Enforcers for Thirdport."

This little twerp with the black eye and cuts and bruises on his neck and hands was an enforcer? A *head* enforcer? He barely came up to Torr's chin. "What's going on?" Torr didn't wait for his answer before stepping around him and pulling Castra up into his arms. They stood looking at the small man.

"Are you familiar with 43035KPS?"

Torr looked down at Castra who quietly said, "Kat."

"Yes. Why?"

"41219DGP?"

Annoyed he looked down at Castra again as she shrugged. "No, not by formal ID. Do you have a name?"

"Davd Palfy."

Fratz, he could have gotten more information out of the couch Castra had been seated on at this rate. "I do not know anyone by the name of Davd Palfy. *Why?*" When there was no immediate answer, Torr decided to push. "Well, *Head?*" the smaller man winced at that. Torr almost ignored the movement but this jerk was being a prick. "You didn't give me a name, remember?"

"Cal," the man bit out and Torr nodded.

"Thank you, Cal." Tor didn't quite hide the sarcasm in his voice. "What's going on? Kat lives in Centerport. She's an enforcer there, reporting directly to Head, so if you need information—"

"She is no longer an enforcer."

"What are you talking about? Is she okay?" Castra asked immediately.

Cal turned away from them but Torr grabbed his arm stopping him. He could take this little schmuck and none of the other enforcers in the room seemed to mind. At least no one was coming to the man's defense. "I think Castra deserves an answer after you come in here and scare her to death. What's wrong with Kat?"

"I'm afraid that's classified."

"Fratz if it is!" He turned to Castra. "Get your mem on line."

For the first time Cal's face showed unease under the arrogance. "What?" Castra leaned slightly against Torr. "Mem? Is something wrong with her? What's going on?"

Cal motioned for his men to leave the apartment and finally turned to Castra. "There's some confusion." He kept talking though Torr opened his mouth to interrupt. "Puter shows that Kat Stans and Lil Stans boarded the shuttle from Centerport yesterday evening for the trip to Thirdport. We are unable to locate them at this time."

"Unable to...That's impossible." She quickly pressed her gimp for the familiar link to her mem.

Cal shook his head but seemed to be waiting for an answering ping along with them. No acknowledgement came through her gimp. After what felt like a very long wait, Cal silently inclined his head to them and headed for the door.

"Cal!" Torr reached for the smaller man again but Cal avoided him.

"I don't have any other information for you. If you hear from your family, you are under orders to contact enforcer headquarters immediately." Without another word, Cal let himself out of the apartment.

Torr turned back to Castra and at the sight of her tears took her into his arms. "Try your mem again."

"She would have answered by now, at least a wcb if she were busy."

"Then try Kat."

She took a steadying breath and pinged her niece. Again the interminable wait before she faced Torr. "What should we do?"

"Is there someone else you could contact? Someone who might know what's going on?"

"Kat's friend, Bree. She might know something."

"Try her."

They exchanged uneasy glances as the third attempt to locate someone went unanswered. That was unprecedented in Torr's experience. Sure, you might not get an immediate answer but there had always been a response of some kind acknowledging that the receiving gimp had gotten the ping.

"Could my gimp be damaged?" The hope in Castra's voice was painful to him. Torr hated to squash that hope.

"Ping me."

She did and there was no delay. His own gimp received the alert instantly. His response was received as quickly and Castra wilted beside him.

"Have you checked to see if there's a message from anyone?"

Castra check her gimp then moved over to the wall display. After a moment Castra turned back to Torr. "Nothing. What could be happening?"

"I've never heard of anything like this. Come on, I want to find Roch."

Castra blinked at that but nodded. Torr and Roch had grown up together. Roch was the only Enforcer besides Kat, Castra really knew. He *would* talk to Torr, regardless of any regulation. They had been friends forever. She and Torr needed to know what was going on.

"His home?"

"No. I don't think anyone should know we've contacted him. This situation sounds like it could be dangerous for all of us."

"Dangerous?" Her voice had gone up an octave.

"Something weird is going on. Cal, for all his presence, is apparently a Head Enforcer. I know where Roch likes to eat. Let's try that first."

Castra only nodded and let him pull her into his arms for a moment.

****

Other books by Donna Steele

Sci-Fi/Paranormal
Alien Embrace
Learning Trust
Wraith's Heart
The Melting - The Infection
The Melting - The Progression
The Melting - Cohesion

Small Town Romance
Homecoming
Red Shoes
Mac's Family
Dance Partner
Nowhere for Christmas
Christmas Present
Christmas With Family
Welcome Home

Made in the USA
Charleston, SC
22 January 2016